Family: Ties that Bind

By Maggie Whittemore

All rights reserved.

Pam Grant publishing copyright pending.

2023

I book is dedicated to the love of my life.

(Forever, for always, and no matter what)

NEVER TRUST A THOMPKINS

Chapter 1

The courtroom fell silent as the judge brought his gavel down. It was done. Everything he had worked for, fought for, all the hardships his little family had endured, were all for naught. It was gone. All gone. That skunk snatched it up like he was buying a piece of penny candy. *What does he care if he is ruining my life?* At least they still had the homestead and the ten acres surrounding it, but what good was that? They cannot make a living from so little land. How was he going to provide for his family? His wife, always at his side, kept reassuring him God would provide for them. *Well Lord, how*? He thought. *How am I going to do this?*

He had prayed hard for a solution before the bankruptcy hearing. All he was asking for was another chance, just one more chance to make the farm work. He knew he could do it. God had let him and his family down this time. It was so hard to know what His intentions are when you simply cannot understand why on earth, He would let his God-fearing family suffer this kind of blow. His family clung to him. They looked at him for answers. What could he tell them? How could he look into the faces of his children and wife and pretend this was going to be, OK? He knew he was a broken man.

He didn't feel well. His stomach churned, his head ached, and his chest hurt. After all, his heart was broken, his dreams gone. Why wouldn't he feel well? Zack Fern looked at his wife. She cradled their baby son in her arms. How proud he had been the day little Zackary was born. He considered her eyes and saw despair. Tears streamed down her face, and he had no words of comfort for her. His daughter, Judy, also looked at him. She was turning into such a beauty. Just like her mother. She was a bit headstrong, but in this world that might just do her well. He placed a hand on her shoulder and gave it a reassuring squeeze. My, how the good Lord had blessed him with such a wonderful family. And now he could think of nothing more than them and how he could make this mess better.

That skunk, Thompkins, started over toward them. He was likely coming to gloat. Zack wouldn't give him that satisfaction! He took his wife by the hand and quickly exited the courtroom. He found that as he walked down the stairs to the ground floor, he became tired. *How odd.* He thought *why he was only thirty-eight*. Hardly old and yet just the stairs seemed to be a chore. No doubt a result of the horrible day, but he found himself praying he could just get home to rest. Such an odd thing, he thought as he prayed that prayer. *Why would I pray to "just get home?"*

As he and his family reached the bottom of the stairs, he began to feel a sharp pain in his chest. So sharp was the pain that it momentarily took away his breath and he stopped for a moment to make sure he could regain his air. His wife looked at him, concern, and panic flashing over her face. Before she could say anything, he said, "I am fine. Let's get home." He headed for the door that led into the small town.

His daughter was slightly ahead of them as he exited the building. At seventeen, she was such a beauty, his pride and joy. He was still on the porch of the courthouse when his legs gave out. He simply crumpled to the floor like a rag doll. He knew then it was his heart. God was calling him. Not now, Lord, he pleaded. My family needs me. This is not my time. But he knew it was. How would they survive? What a poor job he had done as a man. He knew God would likely admonish him for this failure, but what could he do?

He heard his wife scream. He saw a crowd gathering around him. His vision was beginning to get fuzzy on the edges, as though he was looking through a hole in a fence board. *How odd*, he thought. As the hole he saw through grew smaller and smaller he saw the face of his beautiful daughter. Tears streamed down her face, and she was saying something, but he couldn't hear her. He realized he heard nothing. The sounds of the bustling town were suddenly gone. He mustered what little energy he had left and said in as big a voice as he could muster, which was little more than a whisper, he surmised, "Never trust a Thompkins!" His daughter heard him. He knew she had. And then he was on his way to heaven.

Amongst the screams and the tears, the town doctor came running up to aid Zack Fern. Zack and his family had been here for several years, and the doctor knew them all well. Not that they got sick much, but they were always there for church and all the town picnics and always ready to help a neighbor in need. Good people.

As soon as the doctor saw Zack's face, he knew he was too late, but for the sake of the family, he went through the routine to make sure. Zack Fern was dead. His heart had burst. The doctor had seen it before and knew what to look for. He looked at Zack's wife and crying children and had to say the words he hated to say. "I am sorry Mrs. Fern; Zack is with the Lord now." She fainted, and two of the men surrounding the scene caught her. Thankfully, she had already handed off the baby to a local woman to hold while she attended to her husband.

"Take her to my office please," the doctor said rather matter of factly, "Judy, go with your mom. I will be right there to give her some smelling salt. And take your brother too please."

Once the Ferns had left, the doc looked at the people standing nearby. He knew them all, had even brought some of them into the world. "Take him gently boys," said the doctor, "and put him in the icehouse for now. I will send for Will to make a casket."

Will Tasker was the finest casket maker around. He took his time and always made a lovely pine box, even for those who really couldn't afford to pay him for it. He was a good man.

Knowing the circumstances surrounding the bankruptcy- in small towns everyone knew everyone's business- the doctor knew that they would be able to afford little to pay Will when he was finished.

"Better call the preacher too boys," said the doctor. "I best be attending to the Widow Fern now."

Doctor Todd hated that he was usually the first person to call someone a widow or widower. Part of the job he simply didn't like much, like what he had to do now. He knew when he brought Mrs. Fern from her faint; he would have to give her something to calm her nerves. He was not wrong.

The funeral was on the following Saturday. It had been a rather wet end of winter months this year, and it was raining again. The entire town turned out on this rainy Saturday, everyone except the Thompkins family. Doc Todd had told them not to attend. Given the state the widow was in, he thought it best if they didn't come to pay their last respects. Brad Thompkins, Peter's boy, seemed more upset than the rest of them. It didn't quite make sense to the doc, but, given the last few days, very little made sense.

As the crowd stood in the deluge of rain, Ben Todd thought about the recent loss of two patients. Zack Fern had been the first loss and there was little Ben could have done about that even if he had been standing right next to him. The heart attack Zack suffered was swift and powerful. God had called him and there was nothing else to it, but the other death bothered him. It had been a child. Little Marie Stockingham had come down with bad influenza and while he had tended her for forty-eight hours, she too was called to be with our Lord. He had tried, tried hard, but in the end, all his medical knowledge proved not to be enough to save the baby girl. Her funeral was to be tomorrow after church.

How gracious, he thought, of the Stockinghams to have attended Zack's funeral seeing as how they had just lost their child. Ben knew that Zack had given them a great deal of help to get their land ready for planting last spring when they arrived in town and, he guessed, this was their way to repay him.

Pastor Tolle was just getting to the part about ashes to ashes when Ben realized his mind had wandered. He waited his turn to grab a handful of muddy earth and toss it down onto the casket. *Will Tasker had outdone himself*, he thought as he laid eyes on the casket. *It's lovely.*

Ben waited and asked Judy if she would like him to take her and her mother home. "We will walk thanks doctor Todd. I think it will help my mother clear her head. The baby is home with a neighbor. He is looking a bit flush and coughing this morning. I am sure it's nothing but decided not to take him out in this rain."

"Good thinking. But are you sure you don't want me to take a look at him?"

"I am sure it's just a cold. You know all this damp weather lately." Judy said rather unconcerned.

"Just the same," the doctor said, "I will be out in the morning to check up on you and your maw and look at that baby too."

"As you wish," Judy said, and she turned to leave through the rain with her mother.

Chapter 2

The bodies piled up. This wouldn't do. It wouldn't do at all.

"Ok Jud, take them outside. All of them. We must begin burning them. This is spreading too fast now."

"Oh Lord, are you sure Doc?" asked Jud Nelson the local handyman and general hired labor in the town.

"Yes, I am sure. Hurry: there will be more coming into town as this spreads. We will make the courthouse our isolation ward for now. It's the biggest building we have. If you see someone coming into town with sick folks, send them there. I will get a couple of ladies from town to help get things set up. Hurry now man, there is no time to lose! And get your mouth and nose covered with a rag! It may not help but it surely can't hurt."

Doctor Ben Todd was smack dab in the middle of the worst outbreak of influenza he had ever seen in this small town, or for that matter, his entire career. This was bad, REAL bad. People all through town were ill. He had been so busy with all the sick folks in town that he hadn't had time to check on anyone in the outlying areas. He prayed they could fend for themselves. Not that there was much he could do other than give some laudanum for the pain and try in vain to keep the fevers down to some sort of less deadly numbers. Now that the laudanum had run out, all he could do was apply cold cloths to their foreheads and listen to them be in pain and suffering. Why was modern medicine not able to cure this??

"Lord, give me some clue what I can do to help these good people." His prayer was spoken aloud but the silent dead in the icehouse didn't hear his plea any more than it seems God did. As many years as he had been a doctor, it never ceased to amaze him that a person could be alive one second and gone the next. Just like that. Sometimes he could intervene and sometimes he was helpless. Today, this whole week, he had been helpless to do a thing.

Where would it stop? When would it end? The sick just kept coming. Whole families were being wiped out. Lord, help me," He pleaded silently. "Lord, help me."

Judy was doing the best she could. At least the sun was shining today. Her little brother Zackary passed away late last night, or was it this morning? She wasn't sure. She looked at her father's watch and saw the time. Yes, last night. She had placed his little body wrapped in a blanket in the barn in a trunk for safekeeping till she could figure out what to do.

Her mother moaned. She was in so much pain. No wonder little Zackary had cried and wailed so during his illness. He couldn't tell us of his pain, but my mother could. Judy had never seen her mother so ill. Sara Fern was not one to let illness take her off her feet, but this was different. She burned with fever; her body wracked with almost constant waves of pain. Moving was almost excruciating for her, yet she was in constant movement.

Judy tried to keep a cold compress on her mother's forehead. She tried to get her to take sips of cool water from the well. Nothing was a comfort to her mother at this point who had been ill since Sunday with this illness. The fever caused her to go in and out of delirium. She spoke to her husband who they buried the day before she became ill. She cried out for Judy who could not convince her she sat beside her. She talked gibberish most of the time, and Judy struggled to understand or make sense of her words.

Judy was tired. Bone tired. She had been caring for both her baby brother and her mother for days. Alone, she had to do the best she could. She tried to remember the times she had been ill and all the things her mother had done to make her well. None of those things seemed to help now.

Where was Doc Todd? He was supposed to have been out here days ago to "check-up" on the baby and maw. Judy wanted to be mad at the old doc but knew him well enough to know that if he didn't come as he had promised there was likely a very good reason. It made little difference now. Little Zackary was dead. He simply took his last ragged little breath and then stopped.... just stopped. Judy cried as she wrapped him in a blanket and took him to the barn. She didn't want her mother to see him like that. She wasn't sure what else to do but put him carefully in the barn. She placed him in an old trunk they had used when they moved here and closed the lid so nothing would disturb his final slumber. Once he was gone, he looked so peaceful, angelic even. She envisioned he was being cradled in Jesus' arms. That made her feel a bit better.

She really had little time to mourn. The animals needed tending, her mother needed caring for, there was food to prepare, water to lug, and wood to fetch. She was just seventeen but knew what was expected of a woman her age. Why, some girls she attended school with had quit school and gotten married at sixteen, some even at fifteen. Some even had babies of their own. She was, near' bouts, the oldest person at her school. She thought about all the work she would have to make up when she got back to classes. What with the time she missed after her father's death, and now here with the family to take care of there had been little time to even think about school.

While she cared for her little brother, she imagined that he was her baby. What total grief it is to lose a child. She knew that now. She wanted children of her own, but there were no boys interested in her that weren't worth a hoot. She kinda liked one boy, but quickly pushed the thought from her mind. After what had happened, well that would simply NOT be an option. Never! Never! Never! a possibility for her.

"Silly daydreaming girl!" she said to herself aloud.

The words spoken out loud startled her mother's light sleep, and immediately Judy felt terrible for disturbing her. She went out to feed and water the livestock, and then she would gather up some water for the day and some wood and make some breakfast. Today she HAD to get some laundry done as she figured that clean clothes and blankets would help to keep the sick bugs from breeding as fast. She wasn't sure it would help but she had to try.

She went about getting all the stock tended to for the morning and got some water gathered up for the day and the wash. She went back in to find her mother sleeping. She hadn't really slept for days, so Judy was glad she was finally able to get some rest. Perhaps this was a sign she was getting better. Judy prayed this was true. She prepared some oatmeal as that was easy to warm up for her mother when she finally awoke and ate her bowl with a glass of goat's milk. Mary, her goat, was such a fine milker.

After breakfast, she sat down in front of the fireplace in her mother's rocker and decided to read a bit to give her mom some more time to rest. She wanted to check to see if her fever had broken yet but didn't want to disturb her, so she kept her distance for a little while longer. Luke: that seemed like a good place to read, he was, after all, a physician. Perhaps she would gain some divine insight that would help her to care for her only remaining family member, so she began to read.

When her eyes fluttered open, she realized she had dozed off. What time was it? She couldn't tell by looking outside although it was light out, the sky was filled with dark clouds and a cloud-like misty rain surrounded the cabin. Now that the cabin was a bit lighter, she took a good look around the cabin. Oh my, she did have work to do. *What a silly child she was*, she thought, *no time to be sleeping while all this work needed to be done.*

Then she saw her mother's face partially lit by the daylight from the windows. Something wasn't right. She looked like a porcelain doll. Her eyes were open, but they were glazed looking and her skin was so pale. Beads of sweat still clung to her temples, and her hair was matted to her head.

Judy just stood there, staring at her mother. She stood there for what seemed like an eternity but likely was only a short time. She slowly walked toward her mother. "Maw", she said in a soft voice. "Maw!" a bit louder that time.

When her mother didn't respond either by sound or movement Judy took a step closer. White foam leaked from the corner of her open mouth and Judy knew.

Her mother was dead.

Judy had spent hours (or was it days) sitting on the floor staring at her mother's body lying on her bed. She thought nothing, ate nothing, spoke nothing, and didn't even cry. She just sat, staring, bewildered, and confused.

When she finally became aware again, she knew she had work to do. She covered her mother with a spare blanket and went out to the barn. Without glancing in the direction of the trunk her brother was in, she grabbed a spade and headed for the grassy patch near the edge of the woods. Alone, she wouldn't be able to bring her mother into town, but she could give her brother and mother a decent burial. It was the last good thing she could do.

She paused at the door when she saw that the livestock had no water or food. How long had they been without? She wasn't sure but went about the business of getting them all set before she undertook her unhappy task.

The ground was soft, the rain and dampness had made the soil a mucky, muddy mess. This would not be easy. She was determined to do a good job. She spent hours digging the two graves. Her brother's grave was easier. So small, but she made it big enough to put the whole trunk in the hole. It wasn't pretty but at least he would have a casket. Her mother, well she would think about that one, but for now, she made the hole plenty big and deep.

She remembered that her father had told her once, when they went to a funeral in town, that they had to make the hole deep to keep critters from digging up the dearly departed and eating them. She was determined that would never happen to her family! When she figured the hole was deep enough, she went a little deeper. So deep in fact, that she had a hard time getting out of her freshly dug hole.

She fashioned a couple of crosses to place at the head of the graves. They were not as fancy as those in town at the cemetery, but it was something to mark that their final resting place was here. Later, when she had a bit more time, she could put their names on them. Judy was unable to find the makings for a casket for her mother, so she did the best she could. She wrapped her in the new material her mother had tucked away to make herself a new Sunday dress, and then in the thickest blanket she had. Her mother looked so pretty, draped in that new material. How her father would have loved his wife in that color. It was his favorite after all, and that was why her mother picked it.

When she had finished with the preparations, she got the small wagon that she harnessed Mary, the goat, to during harvest time. She hitched Mary up and led her to the front door. She wasn't sure if Mary could pull her mother's weight, but Judy figured if she could pull a cart full of potatoes, she should be able to help her with her mother's body.

Judy struggled with the weight of her mother's body. Eventually, she had most of her mother on the cart. Mary had a bit of a hard time getting started but with some help, Judy and Mary got her mother to the site. She offloaded the body and took Mary back to the barn and got her and the other animals in for the night. The sun was setting, and it wasn't safe to be out after dark for them. She carried her little brother, trunk, and all, to the site and carefully put him down beside his mother.

She thought she should have put them together, but it was too late for that now as it would soon be dark. She got the bodies in the graves, read several passages from the Bible. Psalms 23, several sections of Romans 8, and a bit from Timothy 2, and sang a chorus of "Swing Low Sweet Chariot" and began to fill the dirt in on the last of her family.

It was well past dark when she finally finished. She could hear the coyote or perhaps wolves in the distance. She could never really tell them apart. Her father was the one who was good at that. She went into the cabin. Drank some milk, ate a slice of bread, and crawled into her own bed for the first time in days.

She slept till late the next day.

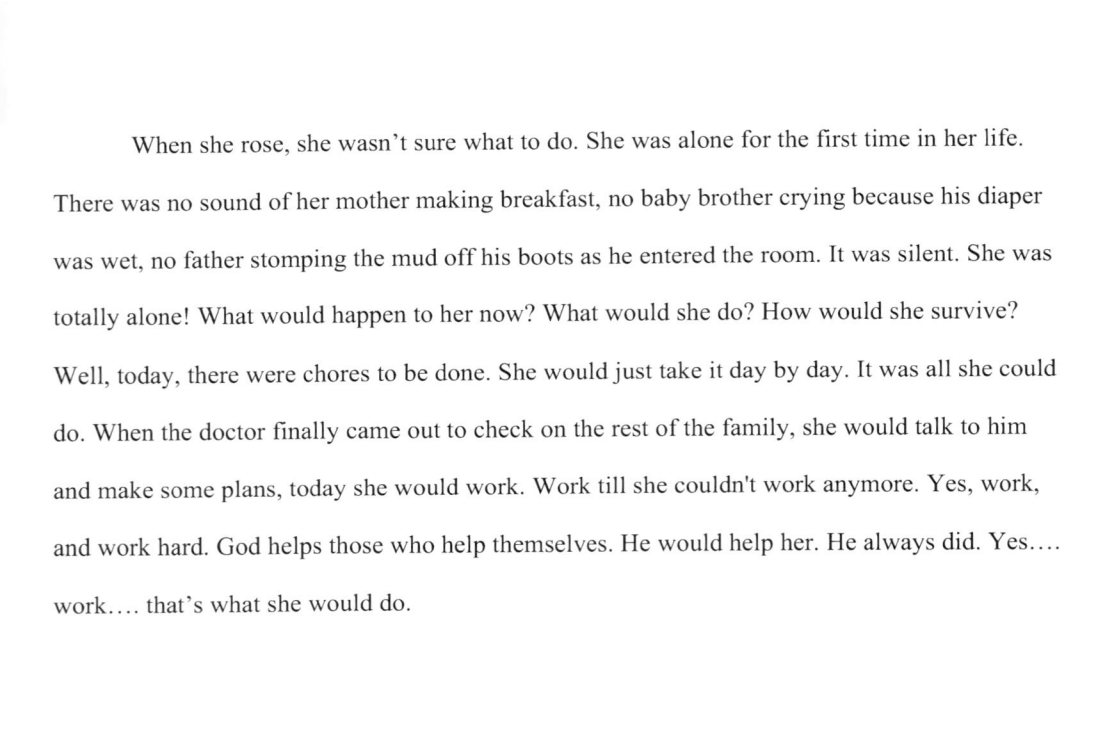

When she rose, she wasn't sure what to do. She was alone for the first time in her life. There was no sound of her mother making breakfast, no baby brother crying because his diaper was wet, no father stomping the mud off his boots as he entered the room. It was silent. She was totally alone! What would happen to her now? What would she do? How would she survive? Well, today, there were chores to be done. She would just take it day by day. It was all she could do. When the doctor finally came out to check on the rest of the family, she would talk to him and make some plans, today she would work. Work till she couldn't work anymore. Yes, work, and work hard. God helps those who help themselves. He would help her. He always did. Yes…. work…. that's what she would do.

Chapter 3

Hours turned to days; days turned to weeks. Judy kept herself very busy trying to get past her grief. It helped, until night when it was quiet, and she was alone. At those times, the sorrow, and memories of all the death she had witnessed came flooding back to her. She tried to make herself so tired at the end of the day that there would be no room for anything but sleep. Sleep, however, eluded her most nights.

She learned that the reason she had never seen the doctor. It was because there had been an influenza epidemic in the town. More than half the town had fallen victim to the disease and others were still coming down with it. Old Man Macdonald had told her from a distance while he rode by. He waved her off when she began to come close to him.

"Don't come near me missy," he said in a yell. "I might be infected. The wife and 2 of my boys have passed from this plague."

He then went on to tell her about what was happening in town. The bodies were being burned so as to control the growing number of dead. The town hall and church turned into makeshift hospitals, and bodies littered the roads of those who hadn't made it to town before losing the battle for life.

Judy told him about her little brother and her mother. And that she had tended them best, she knew how.

"I am mighty saddened to hear that news, Judy," he said lowering his head, "You stay put for a while longer. Things are not better in town yet. Wait till you see people on this here side road and ask them how town is before you go venturing in there on your own. You listen good now girl, it might just save your life."

With that, Mr. Macdonald began to head back toward his farm, which was on the other side of the creek and a few more miles down the road. As he rode away, Judy thought she heard him cough. That same croupy cough her mother had started with. She wondered if she would ever see him again. She heeded his words and stayed at her farm for weeks.

Spring turned into early summer, and before long she found another traveler who told her the illness was over. He, and others like him, went home to home trying to find those who passed alone in their homes and also those who tried to make it to town and didn't. She let him know about the meeting with Mr. Macdonald, and the man said he knew where his place was and would check in on him.

The other news he told her was that the doctor. had caught the illness toward the end of the epidemic. Evidently, the long hours of tending all those souls in the town had run him down so that he fell ill and became the town's last victim.

Astonished at that news, she asked who else that she might know had passed. After some thought, he began to name names of those who he knew she might have known. The list was long,

Dr. Ben Todd,

Will Tasker and all his family,

the Stockinghams; the whole family,

Jud Nelson,

Peter Thompkins and his son,

Judy's head popped up when the mention of the Thompkins was made.

"Which son?" she questioned "Which one of the boys?"

She had gone to school with some of them but in her head and her heart she could hear herself praying it wasn't Brad. She had always liked him. She had even envisioned them together one day when she was a silly adolescent schoolgirl. Now, of course, that was a preposterous notion. Especially given what HIS family had done to HER family.

"The eldest one, Tommy is his name I believe, he had been away at school and came home when he heard his daddy was ill. He never made it back to school though."

"Oh," she said rather flatly, "Thank you for all the news. Would you like something to eat or drink before you continue your grim task?'"

He tipped his hat and shook a cordial no and headed on his way toward the homes that were dotted beyond her home. There were not many, and she knew that he would likely find others who were not as fortunate as her mother and brother to have someone survive to bury the dead.

She would wait a few more days before venturing into town. She didn't want to see bodies anymore and figured she would wait till all signs of the epidemic were over.

That afternoon she sat in her mother's rocker outside the homestead with a cup of cool water she had drawn from the well. She watched a rider coming up the road and was surprised to see that it was a face she recognized. She started to smile at finally seeing a friendly face but quickly scolded herself and put on a staunch stoic face as Brad Thompkins rode closer.

"Judy, I came to see if you and your family were ok. No one in town has seen any of you for some time and, well, I was worried you might all be ill." Brad said without dismounting from his massive steed.

"I do thank you for your concern, Mr. Thompkins. I am fine, and my little brother and mother are buried outback near the woods, if you care to pay your respects. I am sorry to hear of your family's loss as well." She said rather cold and matter of fact like.

Brad hung his head and quietly said, "I am sorry Judy, I truly am."

"I am sure I will be just fine Mr. Thompkins and I would appreciate it if you would address me properly as Miss Fern." Her words were harsh and cutting and she didn't mean them to be so sharp, but it was said, and it was done. *No sense worrying about that now*, she thought.

"Yes ma'am," he said and turned his horse and began to ride away. He had another thought it seemed and turned back to stare at her for a few seconds, only to turn again and ride away at a fast pace back toward town.

Well, she thought, *I guess I told HIM!*

Chapter 4

Judy rose early the next day and was glad the weather was warm, and the sun shone brightly. She went about her morning chores, and after letting out the stock, she milked Mary, the goat, and made herself a hearty breakfast. Today she would go to town.

She took the shortcut through the woods that she so enjoyed. The birds singing and the creek babbling over the rocks gave her heart a short burst of joy that it had not felt for some time. She finally emerged from the cover of the woods to find the road all to herself. It wasn't until she had entered the town that she saw another wagon. The town seemed like such a sad place. People that were out in town, and there were not many, hung their heads and looked at the ground for the most part. The store was quiet, and Mrs. Pringle waved at her as she passed by. She found Pastor Tolle at the cemetery erecting a pile of crosses that lay at his feet.

"These are all those who didn't get a Christian burial," he told her. "The fires," he said with a look in his eyes that told her it was a horrific sight that he had sadly beheld.

"I am sorry," she said and walked away, glad she had not witnessed the sights and sounds that those who had been in town had. She still could smell a faint smell of burned flesh, or she thought she could, as she walked near the other end of town. She quickly changed direction and began to walk by the stores and offices that made up that side of town. When she got to the only bank in town, she smiled at the man in the window who looked at her a might oddly at first then waved her in.

She went into the bank. She had never been inside a bank before. Her father always made the rest of the family stay outside or at the store when he had dealings with the banker. It was a strange place, she thought as she walked through the doors. The bars in parts of it made look more like some sort of jail than a place to keep your money.

"You're Miss Fern, aren't you? Zack's little girl?" the banker asked with a crooked smile on his face.

"Yes sir, I am. Judy Fern is my name."

"Where is your mother girl, I need to speak with her, and it's urgent. Go get her and tell her that I need to have her come and see me today." The banker spoke to her as though she were a five-year-old.

That just made Judy's blood boil when people treated her as some sort of inferior being. "I am sorry, Mr., umm, Mr. What was your name again?"

"Peel young lady, Daniel G. Peel is the name," the banker said as though that was supposed to be something special.

"Well," Judy began, "Mr. Peel, I am afraid you will not be able to talk to my mother as she has passed away in the recent sickness that befell this town. As a matter of fact, I am the sole survivor of my entire family, so, sir, if you have something to say regarding my family, I do wish you would get on with it so that I can be about my way." She felt quite sure she had stated that in a rather adult and stately manner. She would not let this self-important man get the best of HER!! *There goes that pride thing again*, she thought. Mamma warned her about letting that get the best of her, as her daddy was fond of saying, "People should talk down to other people less they have a reason."

"AHHH I see, "he said with a long pause. He looked Judy up and down and then told her to have a seat. "I am sorry to hear of your family's misfortunes Miss Fern, but I need to discuss some financial issues with you."

Well, Judy knew little about their family's finances as her father didn't discuss those things with the family. She was sure that he did with her mother, but surely not with the children. She stared blankly on while the banker talked about loans, payments, forfeitures, collateral, and other terms that meant little or nothing to her.

Finally, when she thought, she could listen to it no more without her head spinning off like a top, she heard the words that she knew the meaning of. "If we cannot settle this debt your father had incurred, we will have no choice but to take your farm."

Well, that brought Judy right to attention. She paused for a quick moment and asked him how much money her father owed the bank. She was astounded when she heard the amount "$45.00." Why that was a fortune!! How could she come up with that??

"How long do I have to raise this money?" she asked quickly as though every second counted.

"Three weeks Miss Fern, then I will be forced to start the proceedings to take your farm and the remaining land so that it can be sold to pay the debt." He said it coldly like it was the most natural thing in the world to take someone's home and land.

"I will get you your money, Mr. Peel. I will get it to you before the deadline. I promise before God, you have my word on that." Judy rose quickly and turned to find that several of the "good" town folks were milling about the bank and had likely heard of her dilemma. *No matter*, she thought. She would do this. The only problem she had been how. How could she, a young lady, earn that kind of money??

She left the bank and went to the church. She went inside leaving the preacher to tend to his grave markers and knelt before the pulpit and prayed for God to send her an answer. She prayed harder than she had ever prayed in her life. What could she do? How could she survive? "God help me, somehow, someway, make it so apparent to me that I couldn't help but see it!" she prayed. She got up and turned to leave the church. Brad Thompkins was standing in the doorway blocking her exit.

God, she thought, *I asked for help, not HIM!* She quickly apologized to God; she was always having to apologize to people, even God on occasion. Brad began to speak to her when she turned but she put up her hand and stopped him from speaking.

"Mr. Thompkins, I have nothing to talk to you about." she said and began to brush by him.

"Judy, um Miss Fern, talk to Rudy Wellington. He owns the stable here in town. I hear he is in the market for some stock and thought perhaps you might have some extra to sell." he said in a hurry as she turned to go by him without getting to close to his rather large muscular body.

"I will thank you, Mr. Thompkins, to keep your suggestions to yourself!" she said flippantly.

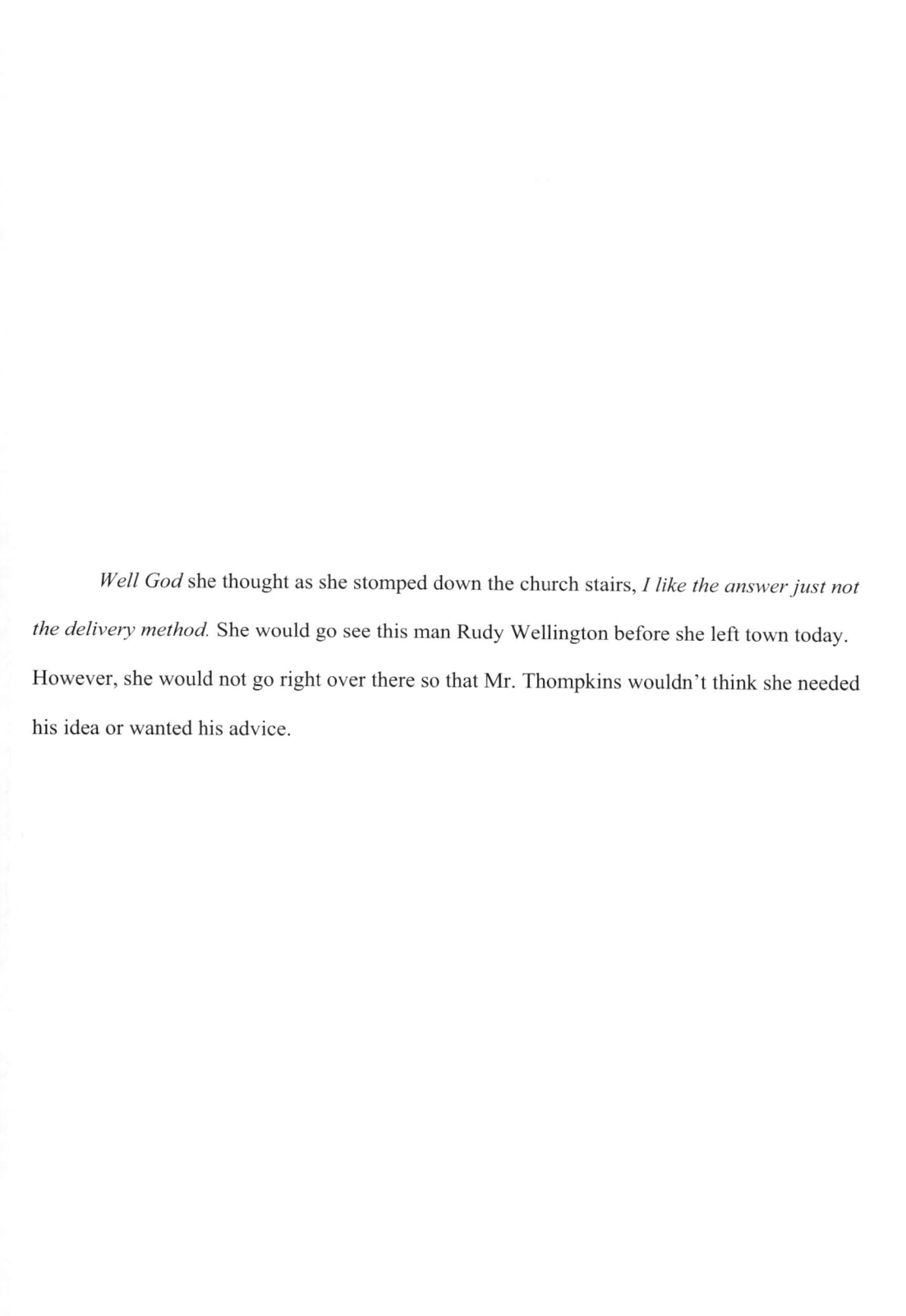

Well God she thought as she stomped down the church stairs, *I like the answer just not the delivery method.* She would go see this man Rudy Wellington before she left town today. However, she would not go right over there so that Mr. Thompkins wouldn't think she needed his idea or wanted his advice.

Chapter 5

Mr. Wellington did indeed want to buy her stock. The going price for cattle and sheep was a bit less than she had hoped, but she sold off all the stock her family had with the single exception of her beloved goat, Mary.

The day the deal was made; Mr. Wellington came to her home to collect her stock with several men from town. He provided her with $50.00 cash money for the animals and told her he would throw in another 50 cents for the old goat, but she said the goat stayed. The men gathered up all the livestock and trotted them toward town.

The homestead got quieter and quieter with each step of the men's horses. Soon it was just her and Mary in the big barn.

Poor Mary was so lonely after that. She had been used to a whole barn full of stock, and now she and Judy were alone. Judy hugged her, and Mary seemed to sense her pain and leaned into her a bit.

Judy cried till no more tears came. She saved the farm. She did it. She would be ok. She had Mary. She and Mary could handle this. They were tough. Practically grew up together. They understood each other. Then all at once, she realized her only friend in the world was a goat. She began to laugh and then more tears came.

By the time morning came, Judy had scarcely realized she had spent the whole night in the barn with her goat. *Winter will be here before long*, she thought, *and we have to be ready. There was much to do, so very much to do.* Today she would begin to prepare.

Judy fed and watered the goat and then got herself something to eat. She harnessed Mary to her little cart and took her to the big field just east of their home. There was very little hay left and Mary would need plenty for winter. Judy took her father's scythe with her to the field. She was a bit shorter than her father but figured she could make it work. She swung the large blade and almost lost her balance as the blade sliced through a large swatch of tall field grass. She widened her stance and kept going. When she figured she had a wagon full she would lay the scythe down and work her way gathering armfuls of fresh-cut grass and loading it into the wagon. Wagon after wagon, she gathered in the field and brought them back to the front of the barn. The horse coral would be her makeshift drying yard. She unloaded each wagon carefully spreading it, so the warm summer sun dried it nicely. When she had brought back 12 or 13 wagon loads and had them all spread out, she realized it was beginning to get dark and unhitched Mary from her wagon and got her bedded down for the night.

She went into the house and drew some cool water from the picture on the table into a bowl. She slowly lowered her hands into the bowl. The water quickly turned a muddy red color as the dirt and blood from her many blisters began to dissolve into the water. She was so tired, so sore, but glad she had a good day's work done. When her hands were cleaner and felt a bit less sore, she applied some of the salve her mother had used for her father's blisters and wrapped them with some clean rags. She didn't bother to eat; she laid down and fell instantly asleep.

When she awoke at about daybreak, Judy found it hard to move. Her arms and hand were stiff and sore. She knew she could stay in bed and rest, but there was more to be done.

"Lord," Judy prayed, "help me to do what I have to do. Guide me Lord so that I don't forget something crucial. Be here with me God. I NEED you. Give me strength."

With that prayer, she rose, still stiff, still sore, but moving. She knew she had to. She would survive. After a light breakfast, she wrapped more rags on her hands to pad them a bit, and then she went out and fed and watered Mary. Judy then checked on the hay. It was drying nicely but wasn't ready yet. She looked up at the sky. No sign of rain, she thought. That was good. Today she would take a break from haying and get some of the vegetables harvested from the garden. She wished now she had spent more time planting and tending the garden. *She would not need as big a garden*, she thought being just herself, but now she scolded herself for not thinking ahead. She gathered those things that were ready and took them into the cabin. She would do as her mother had for years. She would get things ready for winter and preserve them just as her mother had in the sand.

Her father had made cold boxes he called them for her mother. They were filled with fine sand gathered from the side of the sandy streams near here. She took them to the cold corner of the barn, as her mother had always done, and carefully put the carrots and onions she had gathered into the boxes and pushed the cool sand around them. Here they would stay until needed this winter. They would keep from freezing, and they would not rot.

Last year she had begrudgingly helped her mother with winter storage of vegetables, but this year she was proud she knew what to do and how to do it. In a few weeks, other things will also be stored here; potatoes and turnip would be stored in the crocks near the animal stalls. The cabbage she would hang, as she had seen her mother do for years, from the rafters in the barn where they would keep well, and after peeling off the outer dry layers the inner layers usually kept nicely for soups and stews. Corn would be cut off from the cob and dried, as would the beans.

She looked at the garden and wished she had planted more, but it would have to be enough. That was all there was so it would have to do this year. *Next year, she would do better,* she thought.

At the end of the day after weeding the garden and watering those things that needed a bit more growing yet, she turned the hay over to allow it to dry out well on the other side before storing it. Tomorrow she would begin gathering more hay. There will be berries to be gathered and turned into jam, and she would have to find that book of her father's that told about setting small game traps. Yes, she could teach herself to do that. She could hunt rabbits and things like that to dry some meat for winter.

She and Mary would be ok. They would be just fine. "Yes," Judy thought, "I am a survivor. I will make it with God's help."

That night after she did her chores, she sat with a glass of warm goat milk and sat down to learn from her father's books. He only had two books. One was the one she was looking at about hunting and trapping, and the other one was a book of poetry. She once heard her father reading from that book to her mother. He loved her so. Judy was glad he was not around to see how frail she had become from the illness that took her. Pushing those thoughts from her head she forced herself to read and learn. Tomorrow she would fashion a couple of traps and see if she might get lucky and find a rabbit or two. Tonight, she felt very grown-up. Tonight, she thought for the first time in her life, she was an adult, planning out her days according to the seasons, using her time wisely, making the hard decisions and choices. *Yes,* she thought, *daddy's little girl is grown up now.*

Chapter 6

From his vantage point, Brad could see her working. She was driving herself hard. He had seen her working in the field gathering hay, seen her storing vegetables. He watched her as she tended to her beloved goat. Marigold, which was her original name, had been shortened to Mary when Marigold got too cumbersome to say all the time. He had seen that goat the day it was born. They were friends then, back in a more carefree time when they were children.

He had loved her so long now that he really didn't know where it had begun. She was all he thought about. He wanted to run to her, tell her it would all be okay. He wanted to put her up on a pedestal and keep her safe. He wanted to be there beside her, helping her, lightening her load, and brightening her day. He knew that was not going to happen, at least not now.

He was a bit puzzled when he saw her going out of the barn and into the woods with wire, rope, and the few odd tools. When he finally figured out that she was trying to set some snares to catch some animals, he almost laughed out loud. Lord, what was she doing?? She didn't know a thing about setting a snare. She wasn't even setting it on a rabbit trail. She didn't try to cover her scent or disguise the trap, and he was pretty sure the foolish things that she slaved over for hours wouldn't work. He chuckled to himself at her tenacity, however. *She was quite a girl,"* he thought woman; he corrected himself, *so brave, so determined to make this work*. He admired that. *He sure could pick'em*, he thought with a self-righteous smirk.

She wouldn't take his help outright. Perhaps, he thought, he could help her, just a bit. She wouldn't know it was him. How could she ever know? Yes, he would help.

He left her to finish up her daily chores and went to where he knew a warren of rabbits lived. He took out his varmint gun. He hadn't used this since he was a boy and quickly dispatched three nice fat hares. He gathered them up, and under the cloak of darkness, he visited all the snares Judy had set that afternoon. He arranged the rabbits so that it would appear her snares had done the trick and captured and killed the animals. He smiled at the thought as he placed the rabbit in the trap. She would never know. Well, he hoped she wouldn't. She would want to tan his hide if she ever thought it was him.

Before he left her homestead, he peeked in the cabin and found her rocking near the fire with her Bible in her hands. She was reading from Job. Seemed appropriate, he thought, given what she had been through. She must have felt like old Job, being tested by God and sent through trial after trial.

He departed and rode home thinking about other ways he might help lighten her burdens. She would never take money from him. He would never want to hurt her pride. She would barely talk to him! How could he help her to do this, but do it on her own? He puzzled over this one all the way back to town.

He longed for the day when he could hold her and protect her as he wanted to. She was a tough woman, but fragile at the same time. He knew God meant for her to be his. He knew this with his whole heart and soul. Now all he had to do was figure out how to get her to stop hating him.

Well, for now, he would play his games, help her as he could, and watch. He would wait for a day when she couldn't help but talk to him. Wait for a day when she needed him. God would bring them together one day. He knew that. One day, but when……

Brad's father was a proud man. Peter Thompkins had taught Brad to seek a woman who could stand on her own. Judy could do that. His father knew, since Brad was only seventeen, that he would be having Judy Fern as his daughter-in-law one day. It took him some time to warm up to the idea. He wasn't too fond of old Zack Fern, as they had a couple of minor run-ins in town over business dealings, but at church everyone was sociable and at the picnics and dances everyone seemed to get along.

Mr. Fern sure was adamant that his daughter was not up for grabs till she was older. Brad and his father had both tried to talk to him about the two young folks at least getting to know each other at church socials and gatherings where they would be properly supervised, of course, but Mr. Fern would hear nothing of the sort.

After what happened at the courthouse, well, that was bad. Nothing happened that day as it was supposed to. "Dad tried," Brad thought. "He tried to tell Mr. Fern, but he had left the building in a hurry, and then, then it happened. The unthinkable happened."

It had been Peter Thompkins who had paid the doctor and the coffin maker. He felt it was the least he could do. They planned to see the widow Fern, but well, then illness befell the town, and nothing has been the same since. Somehow, he had to make it right. Brad HAD to make things right. He would one day he would, but for now, the rabbits would have to do.

Chapter 7

Judy arose before dawn. She could hardly wait to see if all her hard work and studying had paid off. She finished her chores in record time and then began the mile-long walk to where she had placed her first trap. She brought with her a sack to haul home any game she might be lucky enough to get. She had high hopes but knew her chances were not good her first try out catching anything in her crudely made traps.

The first one was along an old, abandoned fence line that she had discovered one day while out picking berries for a pie her mother was to make. The old, barbed wire, once shiny and new, was rusted now, and the posts were falling down and crumbling. The tree growth around the old fence told Judy that this place had not been cleared for field land for at least 10 years or so. Judy assumed that this fence line would provide a natural line of travel for forest creatures. She had never been taught what to look for in a game trail. That type of thing was something reserved mostly for boys or homely girls who weren't expected to get married. Her father was planning on teaching Zack Jr. all those things when he grew up. She pushed the thought of her father and brother out of her mind while she walked along.

As she neared the site, she strained her eyes to look for the trap she had laid. Her heart leaped and her pace quickened when she saw a small brown and white form lying on the ground. *Thank you, GOD,* she thought, as she came upon the small form of a rabbit lying on the ground. She carefully stroked its fur. So soft. She remembered how to take ashes and brains and tan the hide. She could keep all the hides and then make it into a nice soft cape for herself. Yes, she thought with about as much pride as she could muster. "I would look mighty fine with a rabbit fur cape waltzing into town, now, wouldn't I?" she said aloud to no one in particular.

She removed the thin wire from around the neck of the rabbit, and she noticed a small spot of blood on the pelt. She looked carefully and discovered that this rabbit had been SHOT. She was alarmed at first and looked all around the area for signs of another person, but finally decided that this poor thing was likely shot, and then in its panic to get away from the hunter had run smack dab into her trap. She decided it must be a gift from God and placed the rabbit into her sack. At least she would be able to make a nice stew for supper tonight no matter what the other traps brought. She figured that her trapping skills were ok; after all, it DID catch a rabbit, even if it was a wounded one.

She continued on to her next trap she had set near the stream. Rabbits have to drink; she had said to herself upon settling on this site. She sauntered down to the stream quite pleased with herself. Once again, she found the trap full. *What luck,* she thought, *two rabbits on my first day out! Why I must have really been blessed to have done so well?*

She looked at the little body lying there stiff in the trap and thought how sad it was to take a life so that she might eat, but that was the way God had intended it to be her father had told her. He put all these varmints and critters here so they might help feed his chosen people. Daddy always knew about what the good Lord intended. So much so that sometimes, he would fall asleep in church, and momma always said it was because he had heard that bible verse before.

She removed it from the snare and realized this rabbit also had been shot. Now one, maybe, but two wounded rabbits ending up in her trap was another story. Something was afoot! She could smell a rat! She began to get mad, as she considered who might be playing a joke on her. While she walked to her third and final trap, she wondered what kind of mean-spirited person would do such a thing. Here she was trying to do the best she knew how, and someone was having fun at her expense and making a fool out of her to boot!!

She was not surprised to see the third trap also had a dead rabbit in it. Shot! Who could be so devious? Who could be so mean? Who would want to make her look like a fool to everyone when they told the story of the poor little helpless silly girl? She wasn't about to waste the meat, so she stuffed the hares into her sack. The weight of the three rabbits was a considerable amount in the sack so she slung it over her shoulder. She decided to take a look around before she left the site.

There it was!!!! BIG AS LIFE!! A huge shod hoof print was left in the soft sand behind some bushes. There was only one horse in town big enough to fill those horseshoes. BRAD THOMPKINS!! That HUGE lummox of a horse that Brad rode, had been here and left this rabbit, and it wasn't here alone! She was sure steam was coming out of her ears!

"That, that WEASEL!" she said. That was the worst thing she could think of. She ripped her snare up and stuffed it in the sack with the rabbits and stomped back and did the same with the other two. Why the nerve of him. Making fun of her just trying to feed herself was maddening. How DARE he!? What nerve he had! Why she wouldn't talk to him again unless he was the last man on earth. Nope, she corrected herself…not even then!

Well, Mr. Brad Thompkins, I will keep these rabbits you saw fit to make fun of me with, but you wait. You just wait! I will pay you back, in kind, for your trickery. I sure hope you get a good laugh. Laugh long and hard Brad, she thought, *because one day you will pay for this. One day, soon, you will know not to mess with me. One day, you will get yours.*

"God," she spoke aloud, "I don't think it's fitting for someone to ask you for bad for someone, but Lord, I will ask that one day, you let me get even with that HORRIBLE MAN!! Sorry for shouting at you Lord, I mean no disrespect to you, but that man makes me so MAD!"

She sputtered and tried to think of new harsh things to say to him next time she saw him. She simply couldn't come up with enough cuss words to express her anger. Oh, if her father and mother were still alive, they would have shown him. They would have given him what for and he would have gotten it then. As it was, all she could do was just be madder at him than she was before.

She cleaned the rabbits, but threw the hides, along with the bones, into the woods. She would not be caught dead wearing a rabbit fur cape gotten by the means of a Thompkins! Even the thought made her angry. She salted two of the rabbits and hung them out as she had seen her mother do so many times before, near the fireplace to dry. Dried salted meat wasn't the best in the world, but it sure was a sight better than no meat. She took the remaining rabbit and divided it into two and cooked one half into a nice stew with a few potatoes and some parsnip and a couple of carrots. The other half she tied up in a string ball and baked it off in her smaller cast iron pot over the fire. That baked rabbit would make some mighty fine sandwiches for a few days she thought. Now, she began to construct fresh bread to bake. This loaf of bread got a bit more kneading than it really needed, as she still fumed over that horrible man on the big horse. It would likely be tough bread, but that was ok. She was going to hold on to this anger for a LONG time, a very long time!

Chapter 8

Judy refused to go into town after that for weeks. She was sure everyone would be snickering after that MAN had told what a great joke, he had played on her. No, she had some dignity and pride left, and she wasn't about to give him the satisfaction of gloating. She, instead, worked from sunup to sundown to get in enough hay and gather supplies for the winter months ahead.

All the signs her father used to use to predict a tough winter were there. The paper wasps had built their nests very high in the trees, the squirrels were gathering more food, and building bigger nests of leaves than usual for themselves this year. The husks on the corn were thick, and the spiders were building huge webs and coming into the house much earlier than usual this year. Yes, she knew it was going to be a long rough winter, and she was doing her best to make sure she was prepared.

She gathered hay until there was little decent hay to be had. She had gathered berries and made some jams with the last of her sugar and had preserved all the vegetables she was able to and, had already begun rationing how much supplies she used. She gathered some of the local nuts and roasted them for snacks in the evening as her mother had. She even had caught and dried as many fish as she had time to catch. She was about as prepared as she could be.

However, some of her staples were dangerously low. She knew, by the look of the sky, that she had to make a trip into town soon and get her needed supplies. Some fences needed repair and she was out of nails. She didn't have any livestock now, but that was no reason to let the place go to pot. She would one day get more livestock. Why she envisioned herself one day being the regions only woman cattleman. She could do it. She was determined to succeed and show that haughty, self-righteous, weasel of a man, Brad Thompkins that she wouldn't be beaten down. She often referred to him as Brat Thompkins when she talked to Mary the goat while she was milking her. She snickered to herself every time she said those words out loud. She was sure that Mary not only knew, but agreed with all she was saying.

She and Mary, though close before, were thick as thieves now. Mary became her only friend, her confidant, and Judy loved her greatly. She would spend endless hours outside in the barn paddock with Mary just sitting in the dirt and looking at the land and sky.

Mary had become so used to Judy as her only company that she would follow Judy all over the place without even a lead. As far as Mary was concerned, Judy was her herd. Mary often bellowed loudly when Judy tied her in the barn for the night. Judy found that she had to tie her in the barn, or Mary would be waiting at the door by morning for her to come out. Judy feared the wolves would get her, so she tied her up in the barn at night, and eventually, Mary got used to the arrangement. But, let Judy be late getting to her chores in the morning, and Mary would again begin to bellow. Who needed a rooster to wake up in the morning? Judy had a goat!

This fall saw several of the chicken flock take ill. Judy did her best to nurse and isolate the sickly ones, but 4 had died. The rest seemed healthy. Judy wasn't sure just what had happened to the others, but she would let her broody hen hatch out a few more chicks this spring and increase the flock again.

She arose one morning to Mary's bellowing and knew that she was late getting out of bed. Today she HAD to go into town. She was out of everything, and she would need to spend the day walking to town, purchasing goods, and toting them home again. She knew Mary would not be happy. She would have to tie her in the barn today. If she didn't, that foolish goat would follow her right into town and back.

She rushed about her chores, gathered the little bit of money she had, and grabbed her mother's old worn coat. Hers no longer fit well, and the wind was really blowing today. There was a chill in the air, and she bundled up as best she could. The walk to town was long, but she knew the way well. The sky looked strange this morning. The dark clouds were different somehow than she was used to seeing. The air felt like, well, it was hard to say really. It was cold, yes, but there was almost a tingly feeling in the air like it had been rubbed on a wool blanket and would snap if you touched it.

She counted out her money carefully. She had spent a small amount when the peddler had stopped by during the late summer. She had used one of her mother's best pots to hold the fish she caught, and it rusted badly. She had forgotten to take it in. By the time she stumbled on it again down near the creek, it was in sorry shape. She tried to save it. Did the best she knew how, but it was an old pot that had seen years of use, and this apparently was its last straw. She felt so bad about ruining one of her mother's things that she bought another one. She shouldn't have. The peddler was more expensive than the store in town, and she knew it, but it kept her out of town that much longer, and so, she had parted with the money and got the new pot.

She began the long walk into town. Mary, bellowing in protest at being confined in the barn, could be heard for at least the first twenty minutes of her walk. That goat sure could yell. Judy had even closed the barn doors this morning. She really wasn't sure why, as she rarely closed them, but for some reason, she thought it best to close them today.

As she approached town, her thoughts drifted to thoughts of her parents and brother. How long had it been? She wasn't sure. The months just seemed to pass by so quickly now. She had kept herself so busy there was scarcely time to think much less mourn. Just outside of town, light snow began to fall. She knew she needed to hurry and get home.

Chapter 9

"NEVER TRUST A THOMPKINS!" Her father's last words reverberated in her head as Brad Thompkins drove by and tipped his hat to her. The NERVE of him, after what his family had done to her and her family. She scowled back at him as his wagon moved down the street. She couldn't help herself from following him with her eyes, however. He was, without a doubt, the most handsome man she had ever laid eyes on. Sandy wisps of his shoulder-length hair showed from beneath his hat, and even though he was dressed in a heavy winter coat, you could still see how muscular he was. His face, tan even though it was mid-December, was more than pleasing to the eye.

What a fool you are, she thought to herself, *ogling at him as though he were a prospect for marriage.* She was ashamed of herself for even giving him a second look. It was because of the Thompkins that she was alone and trying to eke out a living here. It was because of him and his family, that her family was all dead and buried in the cemetery just outside of town and back at the homestead. It was because of him that her family's once sprawling 150-acre homestead was now reduced to little more than 10 acres that surrounded the house. Father was right, never trust Thompkins!

She continued down the now snow-covered street as best she could to the general store. She didn't get into town often, and these days, when she did, it was usually out of necessity. She entered the store and took a moment, while Mrs. Pringle was tending to another customer, to warm herself by the woodstove. The cold seemed to be much worse this year than winters in the past. The coat Judy wore, which was once her mother's, was getting worn threadbare and offered little protection from the cold winter wind. The only gloves she had available were her father's leather working gloves, and those seemed to help only for a short time, but it was all she had. Her mother's scarf was a welcome addition to her outfit as it supplied something to wrap her head in and kept her ears from the bite of the frost. She wished now that she had paid more attention to her mother's urging to learn to knit when she had the chance. She had always thought there would be plenty of time, and then ….

Her thoughts were interrupted by Mrs. Pringle inquiring as to her health these past few months. "It seems," she went on to say, "that the influenza was back in the area, and several folks in town had come down with the affliction." Mrs. Pringle talked a blue streak but never let one answer her questions before going on to the next topic of conversation. After letting the storekeeper go on about all the gossip in the area for a bit, mostly to get warmed up by the stove a bit longer, she finally interrupted to say she needed to get two pounds of flour, one pound of sugar, and some nails for home repair. As the clerk went about her business of gathering her items she continued to prattle on.

"The Perkins' youngest boy died last Thursday. You know him, don't you? He would have been the same age as your brother Zackary if memory serves." Mrs. Pringle said.

With those words, the thought of her brother came rushing into her head. She could still picture him, lying in his crib. He was so small and innocent. Oh, how she wanted to be able to tell him how much she really loved him. She had been so proud of herself when she tried to tend him in his illness, only to have him pass away anyway. You never think when you're young that people will ever leave. Her eyes began to tear up, and she quickly removed the thought from her head. She would not show weakness to anyone. Especially this lady, who would in no time, have the whole town knowing.

"Mrs. Pringle," she said, interrupting the string of gossip flowing from the shop keepers' mouth, "If you don't mind, I am in a hurry. Those clouds to the west look like snow again, and I have a long walk home."

Mrs. Pringle was obviously insulted by her statement and went about gathering the rest of her items without a word. Once they were gathered and placed in a sack, she curtly said, "That will be $1.27 please."

Judy handed the shopkeeper the money, careful to count out every penny so as not to make a mistake. Always take your time where money is involved, her parents had told her. Mistakes, one way or the other, can make or break you in the end. When she had finished paying for her items, there was little left. Thirty-four cents were all that remained of the money she had earned from selling off all the livestock last fall. *Well,* she thought, as she gathered up her sack and exited the store, *that flour and sugar will just have to last me the rest of the winter!*

The wind had picked up from the west, and she was sure now that snow was going to make another appearance. She could smell it in the air and feel it in the crispness of the wind. She quickly snuggled down the ends of the scarf into her mother's coat so that it wouldn't fly off her head in the wind and pointed herself in the direction of home.

She had been walking for only about ten minutes when it began to snow again. She knew it would get bad fast, and she picked up her pace. She was still over an hour's walk from home, and she wasn't making good time in the seven inches of snow already on the road. The few tracks the horses had left dwindled as she got further from town, and by the time the snow began in earnest, she was pretty much just following her own tracks she had made this morning. Before long, she would veer off the road to the shortcut she knew through the woods to her home.

The wind and snow had really picked up when she thought she heard a horse from behind her. She turned to see a lone rider astride a massive horse who must have stood 19 hands high. Although she couldn't see the rider's face lowered against the blowing snow and wind, she was sure who it was. Only one horse that big lived in this area and it belonged to Brad Thompkins.

His steady slow pace attested to the weather conditions. She turned her back to the wind and continued forward on the road. She would not give him the time of day, she thought.

As the horse grew closer, she could hear his voice calling to her through the howling of the wind, but she pretended not to notice. "Judy," he called "Judy be careful." She pretended not to hear. Eventually, the horse was right at her heels, and she could no longer continue to let his presence go seemingly unnoticed.

She turned to face the wind and boldly put her face into the wind to look Brad Thompkins directly in the face. The wind whipped snow felt like needles on her cheeks, but she would not give him the satisfaction of seeing it. "You may address me, Mr. Thompkins, as Miss Fern, thank you," she stated rather coldly and as a matter of fact.

"So sorry Miss Fern, but I was concerned for your welfare. I doubted you had sufficient time to make it back to your farm before this storm hit."

His words sounded to her to be dripping with the honey that came from the honeybees in the old oak on the knoll. "I assure you, sir, I am quite capable of making my own way home. You may go back to town and continue to do whatever it is you do, and rest assured your attempt at chivalry is not necessary."

"Come on Judy, ahhh, Miss Fern, let me take you home. This is getting worse, and pretty quick it will be a whiteout. You will never get home in this."

"Mr. Thompkins, I wouldn't take help from you if you were the last man on earth. I am quite capable of getting my own self home. Now, please take your leave of me." With that, she took one more look at his rugged features and turned and once again began to trudge through the snow. She knew he was quite right of course. The storm was intensifying, and she almost couldn't make out the quickly disappearing tracks in the snow that she had laid down this morning, but she would NEVER take help from the likes of him! Why even the thought of him coming all the way out here just made her angry and more determined to do it. What was he up to anyway? They had taken everything but the homestead from her, and she would be sent to jail before she would allow him to have that too!

She began to silently pray to God to help her get through this so that she could show Brad Thompkins that he was NOT needed by her. Her shoes were filled with snow now, and the ice was stuck to the sides of her scarf which made her face even colder. The wind whipped relentlessly at her, and she looked up to find she could not tell where she was. She had lived her whole life traveling this road, but suddenly fear gripped her as she realized that she could see no landmarks, no features of the land, everywhere she looked the snow fell and blew in every direction. The only thing she was sure of was that staying put would be a death sentence.

She took maybe 3 more steps in the knee-deep snow before she fell face-first into the snow. Her burlap sack of purchases went tumbling into the snow ahead of her. She righted herself, brushed what snow she could from the sack, and kept walking to where she wasn't sure, but she knew she had to keep moving.

She walked along for what seemed like hours before her bare legs under her skirt were bright red, and her feet no longer wanted to move. She wasn't sure she could even feel her feet anymore and it was the sheer power of her will that kept her moving. She looked up once again to see a black shape in the distance. She realized instantly it was the big oak that stood like a sentential for years beside the road. Well at least, she thought, she was still on the road, although she didn't know how she had managed to do it.

When she got to the tree, she leaned against it heavily. She had to catch her breath and the lee of the tree made it possible to escape a bit of the wind. She waited a few minutes before she saw another shape through the snow coming toward her from the direction of town. *BRAD!* She thought *why that snake was following her. Probably he was hoping to find me dead in the snow, so he could have my last thirty-four cents! Such a devious and hateful family, why, she couldn't believe they even had the nerve to show their faces in church on Sunday. Why God allow people like that to claim to be Christian is beyond me!"*

Although she wasn't fully rested, she once again began to trudge through the snow toward where she knew the woods lie. Once there, she was sure that the trees would provide her with some protection from the wind and snow, and she would be able to easily get home from there. Her pace slowed, and each footfall became more difficult. The snow seemed to get higher with every small step. All at once, she felt herself falling, and she was unable to catch herself. Into the snow, she went, right down out of sight. She tried to regain her footing, but it was not possible. She simply didn't have the energy. Perhaps, if she just slept here for a little while, she thought. It seemed warm here. The snow around her was as though a warm blanket was over her. Yes, just a little rest, and then she would be fine. As she drifted off, she thought she saw her father hovering above her. "Daddy?" she called in an almost inaudible voice, and then she drifted off into a dark sleep.

Chapter 10

When Judy became aware again, she could hear distant sounds. Her eyes remained closed as her head tried to make sense of what she was hearing. The sounds and smells were familiar, yet strange at the same time. The smells were comforting, and yet also alarming. She began to open her eyes, and her head began to throb. She immediately recognized the fireplace hearth of her home, but how had she gotten herself here? Last she remembered, she was a long walk from home, and it was snowing. Yes, the blizzard. She then became aware of hearing the wind howling outside her cabin, as her eyes closed again, and she drifted off into another round of unconsciousness.

When she awoke again, she was more aware than in the dreamlike state she had previously been in. Her eyes flickered open and again she saw the fire burning brightly in the hearth. She was close to the fire, wrapped up in some blankets. Although she was only feet away from the warmth of the fire, she felt a chill throughout her body. She was home. She could hear her mother puttering in the kitchen, no doubt making something wonderful for supper.

Then all at once, she remembered she was alone. Her mother and baby brother had both died when the influenza hit last spring. She had done her best to tend to them. Tried to make them well, but the fevers took them in just a matter of days. She had buried them outside of the barn near the woods. When Peter Thompkins, Brad's father, had bought our land out from under us for the back taxes owed, my father's poor old heart couldn't bear it, and he collapsed on the steps of the courthouse never to awake again. One bad year and that had swept in and taken what my father had worked so hard for so many years. She was glad that the influenza outbreak had also been claimed by Mr. Peter Thompkins.

But if her mother was really gone, what was she hearing? She was not alone. Someone was here, in the cabin with her. She rolled away from the fire and realized she had little or no strength. It took all the strength she had to just roll her body toward the other end of the kitchen. As she worked to turn over, she realized that the storm was still raging outside. She could hear the ice crystals tapping against the window and feel the force of the wind as it pummeled the cabin. When she righted her body toward the kitchen, a groan escaped her lips. Her muscles protested being used, and she hurt all over.

"Hey, you're awake!"

The voice was familiar yet foreign all at the same time. Then she saw him. BRAD THOMPKINS! In HER home!! She tried to speak, and all that would come out was a "whaaa" sound. He came to her side and began to speak.

"You collapsed, and near 'bouts froze to death too. I am just glad I decided to make sure you got home alright. You have been out for over a day now. Had me right worried I can tell you." He explained, "Here, take a sip of water."

He held a cup to her lips, and she wanted to protest, but the cool water felt good on her lips, and she drank eagerly. The little drink of water seemed to give her some energy, and she weakly said, "Did you…?" That was all she could get out. He seemed to know what she was asking and as he took the cup back to the table he began to speak again.

"I gathered you up and took you here. I would have rather taken you to town, but the storm was getting much worse, and I knew your place was closer. Had to get you out of the storm and warmed up or you might not have made it." He said matter of factly. "I have seen this before, when I was out with the herd a few years back. We lost a good hand to a blizzard not nearly as bad as this one. We didn't find him till thaw."

His words swirled around her head like a tornado. What was he up to? He must have something up his sleeve. If he had let her die, he could have had the rest of her land. Why??? With that thought, her eyes closed again. She was vaguely aware that he was still talking, but she couldn't make out his words. Sleep overtook her again, and she dreamed of sun-filled summer days and picnics by the river with her family. It would always be this way, she thought, always!

MARY! She awoke with a start and sat bolt upright! What about Mary? She realized she was still near the hearth when she sat up and could see Brad sleeping in her mother's rocker on the other side of the room. His chest rose and fell with each breath, and she took a moment to see how peaceful, innocent, and handsome he was. She brushed thoughts of him from her mind and again her thoughts went to Mary, and she spoke the name out loud without even realizing it.

From behind her, a familiar sound came. Marigold, her goat, was in a makeshift pen in the corner of the room, where her brother's crib had been. Why was Mary in the house?? Goats do NOT belong in the house!!!

When all the other livestock had been sold last fall to pay for the homestead taxes and her winter supplies, she had decided to keep Mary, her favorite goat, for milk this winter. She wasn't much of a looker, but she was a good milker and gave her more than enough milk to drink and use in cooking.

"With this storm," Brad, who had awoken, began, "I brought her in. I didn't want to be out at the barn any more than need be in this mess. Still have to go out once a day at least to tend my horse, but at least, milking is easier."

It was then she realized that the storm still raged outside. How long? What day was it? Had he been here this whole time?

Brad seeming to sense her thoughts said, "Three days. You've been mostly sleeping for three days. I have managed to keep a foot trail to the barn. I tied a rope between here and the barn, so I could find the house again. You know, you should have done that in the fall! Don't you know anything girl?" His inflection said he was teasing, but his words instantly brought anger to her eyes.

"Have you...?" she began, but her voice wavered.

"Yup, since Friday last." he said rather forcefully as he rose from the chair and went to the pot near the hearth and began to stir. "You didn't have much around here, but I managed to make a nice vegetable stew for us. Hope you like stew."

She defiantly pursed her lips not wanting to take anything he had a hand in, but the smell of the hot stew won out, and her stomach growled from hunger. If what he said was right, she had not eaten in 3 days she should be starving! As he brought her a bowl of hot stew, she sat up more and suddenly realized she was wearing nothing but her under things. She gathered up the blankets in front of her.

Noticing her embarrassment, "Ya, sorry about that, but I HAD to get those wet things off you, most of your dress was frozen stiff. I swear, I didn't see nothing. I had to get you warmed up Judy. You might have died, and I wasn't having any of that." He passed her the bowl, and she sheepishly took it from him and began to eat as soon as his back had turned.

It actually tasted wonderful. Was he really a decent cook, or had her hunger just made any old sludge taste good? Nope, she decided as she continued to gobble down the stew, this was downright GOOD! Imagine that...a man who could cook.

Again, seeming to read her thoughts, he said "I learned to cook out on the range. Being the baby in the crowd, they usually left me behind to make them supper. Got pretty good at it too, if I do say so myself."

How was he doing that?? *Get out of my head,* she thought, still eagerly devouring the warm stew, *Stop knowing what I am thinking!"* That was maddening, but she had no time for being mad now. She was hungry. He got her a glass of goat milk and took her bowl. She downed the milk in one long drink.

"How much snow," She asked.

"At least two feet, but might be more, hard to tell the way the wind is whipping it all around. Last time I went out to the barn, it was beginning to turn to freezing rain. It shows no signs of letting up anytime soon. I haven't seen a storm like this one in at least 10 years around here. The mountains, sure, but out here? Almost never see it like this. It's like God decided this whole area needed a good whitewashing. "A "humph" escaped her lips. What would HE know of God or what God wanted? Ok, he may have saved her life, maybe, but he had to have had a reason, ulterior motive or some sort of long-term plan in mind. His kind didn't do things out of the goodness of their hearts. They didn't have hearts.

When they were in school, when they were much younger, before he turned thirteen, and went out on the range with his older brothers and father, she had been quite attracted to him. He had even asked her to a church dance once. Of course, her father wouldn't let her go. No proper brought up young lady ever dated before they were fourteen years of age, she was told, even to a church dance. It just wasn't done!

It was then, she realized, she was trapped here. Trapped here with her worst enemy for God knows how long. Marigold and she were virtual prisoners in her own home. "God," she prayed, "deliver me from this horrible man!"

Chapter 11

Once the realization of her situation sank in, the rest of the night passed without conversation between them. She pretended to be asleep for a long time just watching him from the corner of her eye as he tended the fire, cleaned up the kitchen, milked Mary, and went into the storm to tend his horse. She dared not get up, as she had no idea how long he would be.

When he finally did return, he looked like a snowman. He was covered from head to toe in thick, sticky, white snow. His face was red beneath the snow which attested to the fierceness of the storm. He stomped his feet rather quietly, no doubt an attempt not to wake her as he assumed she was soundly sleeping.

Once free from his coat, he hung it next to the door with his hat and sat down to remove his boots. His flannel shirt was wet, likely from where his coat had gapped in the blowing snow. Once his boots were placed by the fire to dry, he removed his shirt and hung it on the chair so that it might also dry.

She had not seen him bare like this since he was a boy, MY, how he had changed. His chest was muscular, and he was truly a sight to behold. She could still see the tan lines from where, in the summer months, he had rolled up his sleeves in the heat, and the warm summer sun had baked his skin to a golden brown. He turned and walked toward the door again, his shoulders broad, and his shape tapered down to his waist in an almost perfect V shape.

He removed a dry shirt from his saddlebag which was hanging on a peg hook by the door and put it on. She wondered why he might have an extra shirt in there. Had he planned this all along? Don't be silly, she thought, he couldn't have planned the storm. Perhaps, having been out on the range for so long, he just kept one "in case" in there.

She watched him for some time before sleep finally overtook her, and she drifted off. Once again to dream of warmer more pleasant days, except this time HE would also invade her dreams. Those bare bronze shoulders glistening in the sun, wet with sweat from a hard day's work. His muscles rippling in his arms as he swung the ax to split wood with one mighty blow into firewood. He was a powerful vision to behold. He was the most beautiful thing she had ever seen. He looked at her and smiled. The kind of smile that says more than hello, it said much more. He set the ax down and walked to her. He spoke.

The slam of the door to the cabin awoke her from her dream. She wrapped the blanket around her and hurried to the window. She could see only hard-packed snow up against the windowpanes. She went to the door and slowly opened it, just a crack, so she might look outside. She could see Brad walking down a path to the barn, but what she couldn't see was the top of the snow. She opened it a bit wider, and the sight made her jaw drop open. The snow was easily seven feet deep. Several days of snowing and blowing had buried them. Was it blown in between the house and barn that deep, or was it that deep everywhere? The one good thing she noticed was that it had stopped snowing. FINALLY!

She quietly shut the door and hurried to get dressed before he came back. Once she had finished with that, she went about making some biscuits for breakfast. The snow had stopped, so that meant he could leave. He saved her life, so the least she could do was send him on his way with a warm breakfast. She had access to the laying hens nest boxes through the cabin. Her father was so smart to build the chicken coop like that, but there were no eggs. The chickens had likely taken refuge in the barn or the woods when the snow began. Biscuits would have to do, she thought. But then she remembered the jars of wild berry jam she had put up this fall. Those would be a nice touch too. She put on fresh coffee and was busily making the biscuits when Brad returned from the barn.

"Well,," he said with a smile on his face, "I guess someone is feeling better this morning."

"Why yes, I am, Mr. Thompkins. I haven't properly thanked you for saving me, so I thought, as a means of saying thank you, I would prepare you a hot breakfast before you leave." she said with a tone of defiance.

He began to laugh. Laugh loudly. She looked at him with a long-puzzled look, and said, "I fail to see what is so amusing Mr. Thompkins."

"Judy, I am not going anywhere. In fact, I doubt I am going anywhere for quite some time, like it or not! Have you looked outside?" With that, he went to the door and flung it open. "Judy there is 7 or 8 feet of snow out there! Even if I did have a mind to try, I couldn't even find the road, much less walk or ride in this. I had to go out and climb up on the roof last night just to make sure the chimneys were safely uncovered. No storm like this has hit here in all my life. We are stuck here, my dear."

She felt a bit foolish. She should have thought about it. He couldn't ride in this, and without snowshoes walking would be out of the question. Still, gathering her wits about her, she calmly closed the door, and said, "Mr. Thompkins please do not refer to me as "my dear". We are not nor will we ever be endearing to each other. However, given our current situation, I will forgo the formalities and allow you to call me by my proper name. I assume you would also allow me to do the same."

"Well," he smiled, "I guess it's a start."

After breakfast, she did the dishes while Brad offered to milk Mary. The funny thing was Mary didn't seem to mind. Mary had never let anyone but Judy milk her willingly. Strange.

"I need to go to the barn to get some supplies I have stored out there." she said putting on her coat.

"I will go with ya."

She wasn't pleased but said nothing. She was not a helpless girl as he obviously thought. After all, she had managed to retain this farmhouse and the surrounding land all by herself. Admittedly, she didn't know how she would accomplish that another year, but she would find a way. She could take care of herself, without the help of Brad Thompkins, no matter what he thought.

She exited the cabin, and instantly the cold hit her face. She noticed that it seemed to hurt down to her bones, evidence of how close to freezing to death she really may have been. She marveled at the snow. It was amazing. She had never in her seventeen years on earth seen such a site. This must be one of those once in a lifetime storms the old-timers talk about in town. As she made her way through the narrow path Brad had somehow managed to keep open to the barn, she thought that it would indeed be a long time before either of them would be able to leave this place. The cloudy skies attested to the still nearness of the storm. She silently prayed it would move off and not begin again.

Once in the barn, she went to check on the small root cellar her father had built on the floor of the barn. She removed the small wooden hatchway and climbed down the ladder. In the dim light, she was able to make out most of the jars on the shelves. She grabbed several and was about to climb up the ladder when Brad's hand popped down through the hole to grab some jars. Judy passed him several jars and then climbed the ladder to once again stand on the barn floor.

While Brad placed the jars into a wooden box that was in the corner of the barn, Judy walked over, and she took a good look at his HUGE horse.

"What is his name?"

"Tiberius, but we call him Ty for short," Brad said with a smirk. "You may not want to stand so close. He doesn't always behave well around the ladies."

Ignoring his warning, Judy walked up and began talking softly to Ty. Ty's eyes widened, and his ears went back, but Judy held her ground and kept talking to him. After a bit, she extended her hand and allowed Tiberius to smell her. With that, his ears relaxed, and his demeanor changed to calm and relaxed. She took a couple steps closer and patted his head. He began nuzzling her hand, and she was amazed that he was such a gentle creature despite his size.

Brad stood in awe of her. She was truly amazing.

Then the horse got wind of something. He again became nervous. Almost at the same time. Brad and Judy heard them too. WOLVES and they were close!

Chapter 12

As soon as the echoing sounds of the wolf howls registered in her brain, the thought *"fear not, for He is with you"* came to her. She wasn't sure if the "he" referred to God or the handsome young man who grabbed the box of jars and hurried to peek out the door leading back to the house. She was somewhat ashamed that she even had such a thought. God had seen her through so much this past year. Her reliance on Him was all that made her move forward some days. Now she was looking at Brad? No, that won't happen!

She pushed past Brad and flung open the door. She then began to march toward the house. It was then she saw them. Faces lined the snow above her head, looking down into the narrow pathway to the house. She froze in her tracks. Instantly Brad was behind her.

"Don't move," he said, "wait till I tell you then run as fast as you can to the house."

He was talking slowly and softly in her ear. *How could she be so ignorant*, she thought. She nodded silently to him as she looked at the faces above her. Then they began.

The noise of their howling was deafening, first one, then another, and then many. How many she wondered? All of a sudden, he took a hold of her arm and said "NOW!" She moved as fast as she could toward the door. They had no more gotten to the door when the wolves began jumping down into the path. She turned just in time to find Brad kicking at a she-wolf as she tried to force her way in. He managed to get the door shut and turned and quickly looked frantically about the cabin.

"Did your father have a gun? Where are the guns?" Brad shouted.

Outside, the wolves frantically clawed at the door. Frozen in a panic it took Judy a few moments to realize what he was saying. "There in the box by the window. ", she finally said.

Brad flung open the lid of the box and grabbed her father's hunting rifle. He loaded it and threw more ammo into his pocket. Then he went to the saddlebags he had hanging near the door and got two pistols. He handed one to her and said, "Can you shoot?"

She stared blankly at him.

"JUDY!" His voice raised, "CAN YOU SHOOT?"

"YYYes." she stuttered, and he shoved the pistol into her hand.

"Now Judy, listen to me carefully," his voice was softer and gentler than before, "I won't let them get you, but I won't let them kill Ty either. He is trapped in the barn, and eventually they will get in there. I have to go out and help him. I am going to have to kill as many of them as I can. They are light enough to stay on top of the snow. They will get in if I don't kill enough of them to scare them off. Do you understand, Judy?"

She looked into his eyes. Finally getting her composure, she said, "Yes, what do you want me to do?"

"Stay here and keep that gun pointed at the door. DO NOT open that door until you hear me at it. No matter WHAT you hear. Do you understand?"

"Ok," she said quietly.

He placed an ear to the door, and when it quieted down at the door the sound of wood scraping against claws and teeth could be heard at the barn door a few feet away. He flung the door open, pointed the gun and fired, and shut the door behind him in one motion.

Through the closed door, she could hear the sound of her father's rifle going off. Then the pistol began to fire. The sound of wolves yipping and growling and snarling all intermingled with the sound of the guns. Just about the time, she thought that he would run out of ammunition, silent. A deafening complete silence took over the cabin.

    She stood; gun pointed at the door. He told her not to open the door, but what if he was hurt? What if he needed her? What should she do?

    She could hear Ty in the barn whinny a bit. Then even Ty was silent.

    She stood staring at the door. Just stood there staring at it. She wasn't sure how long she had been there straining her ears for a sound when all of a sudden, a very loud bang came from the door. Jolted from her trance, she started toward the door then paused, waiting for another sound.

    Another bang and another came from the door. She lowered the gun she still held in her hand, and slowly opened the door.

Chapter 13

There inside the door stood Brad. He had been kicking the bottom of the door as his hands were holding the box of canned goods, they had originally gone out to the barn to get. In his mouth, he had a burlap sack with Mary's grain for the day. Behind him, Judy could see the bloody snow, and her eyes followed the blood trail to the sight of three fully grown wolves piled next to the barn. There was a patch of blood that was also at the top of the snow on the edge of the path. She suspected there was another wolf up there as well.

She could see the deep scratches on the barn door and the cabin door that the wolves had caused with their claws.

Brad went to the table, put the box down, and set the sack on a chair. Judy couldn't help herself, she charged to him, and hugged him from the back. She realized she had never been so happy to see anyone in her life.

She had been so scared. The wolves in the area had always frightened her. Since she was a child, she had been terrified of something like this happening. She had heard stories. She knew all the legends of wolves that did things like this when times got tough. She had feared she would have to go through something like this. Had it not been for Brad, she wouldn't have been able to survive them, and she knew it. "Whoa!" Brad said, obviously startled by her impromptu hug. "Judy, you, ok?" He turned and put both hands on her shoulders.

She hadn't noticed but tears were running down her cheeks. She had never been so frightened in her life. He pulled her into his chest and softly told her, "It's all right now. Everything is alright."

She regained her composure in a few minutes and was embarrassed at her actions. She was not a weak woman. Why was she acting so silly and vulnerable around HIM?!

She began putting away the supplies, and Brad announced he was going out to the barn to skin the wolves "the hides will bring a nice price in town," he told her. She watched him leave and wondered why she was beginning to have deep feelings for him. The man whose family had ruined her entire life, and she felt soft warm feelings toward him. She softly spoke words of apology to her father. "I am sorry Daddy; I am trying not to let you down."

Later that night with a stew made from vegetables and wolf hearts laid at the table, they sat down. Brad began to say grace. "Lord, now you know I am not much of a talking man, but I sure do need to thank you for the fine meal you have seen fit to provide us, and for Judy's regained health and safety. Lord, thank you for allowing me to be here to help Judy when she needed me most, both times!" he added as he opened his eyes and shot Judy a wink. "Amen," with which, he finished his prayer.

Judy opened her eyes and looked him in the eye, "Amen" she said. It was true. He had been her saving grace twice now. She watched as he shoved a spoon into the stew and ate heartily.

"Why did your father take our land? How could he have been so cruel?" She said the words before she knew what she had done.

"Judy, I have been waiting a long time to explain this to you. Thank God, you finally are giving me the chance." He set down his spoon and looked her in the eye. "Judy, my father bought that land for me. Now wait, let me explain, "he said quickly as he could see she was about to blurt out angry words. "See," he went on, "my father knew from the time I was a youngster that I loved you. He knew your father was going to lose that land, and he bought it so that when I married you that land would always be in the family. Problem was before he could get to your paw and tell him that …. well…. he had his heart attack. After that happened there was not a "right" time, then the influenza came, Daddy passed with that, your family passed, and you wouldn't even give me the time of day to explain. I knew there would be a day when we would talk and straighten it all out. I knew God would bring us together. We were meant to be. I just did not know he would bring a blizzard and wolves to do the job!" With that he chuckled and so did she, a nervous laugh.

    He rose from his seat, wiped his chin to be sure all traces of stew that may have been there were gone and went down on one knee before her. "Judy, your Daddy ain't here for me to ask, but I sure would like you to consider becoming my wife. We need each other, like your maw and paw did, like my paw and maw before she died. My daddy knew that. He was trying to do the right thing for me and you, but you just did not know that. Please Judy at least consider becoming Mrs. Judy Thompkins." With that, he searched her eyes. Unable to find the answer in her eyes, he stood, and went back to his chair and began quietly eating his stew again.

She sat in shock for a long time. Her father had been wrong. They were not bad people, they were trying to help him, but he did not live long enough to know it. She was sure he knew it now.

    She picked at her stew for a bit then began picking up. They avoided each other's gaze that evening. Stealing glances in each other's direction, but never letting their eyes meet.

    That night, while she lay in the bed and Brad slept in a bedroll by the fire, she listened to the sound of his calm easy breathing, watched the rise, and fall of his chest. Did she love him? Perhaps she always had?? What should she do? She was so confused. A few days ago, she would have as soon seen him put into ruin than talk to him, and now here they were. Together in her cabin, alone, and he had professed his love for her. This was unreal. This kind of thing doesn't happen, does it? Finally, sleep overtook her.

When she awoke, he was not in the cabin. His saddlebags were gone. She put on her coat after washing her face and headed out to the barn. Ty was still in the barn. He called to her when she came into the room. She wasn't sure where Brad was, but wherever it was, he was on foot. She patted Tiberius on the head, and then went back into the path that led to the house. She could see where Brad had, apparently, scrambled up to the top of the snow. She followed his footholds as best she could and only lost her footing once before she got to the crest of the snow and peered over the top. She saw snowshoe tracks leading away from the cabin and barn. He must have discovered where her father had stored his old homemade snowshoes last winter, or fashioned a pair of his own, but where was he going?

Why was he leaving her alone? Was he angry she hadn't answered him? Was he never coming back? A million questions ran through her mind all at the same time. He must have left incredibly early in the morning because he was nowhere in sight. The tracks of his snowshoes and that of the wolf pack were the only ones visible. Nothing moved, nothing made a sound, it was peaceful, and calm, and really quite beautiful. The sun shone brightly, and the snow which had almost taken her life now glistened like so many diamonds laid out on the vast landscape. The storm had passed, and now the majesty and the beauty of winter had replaced the fierceness of the storm.

She went back into the barn and that was when she realized Ty was HERE! He would return for Ty, no matter what. That was when she noticed that the hides were also gone. The wolf hides had been taken too. What on earth was he DOING? She spent the rest of the day nervously telling herself one reason after another to explain what he might be doing. She had blown her only chance. She knew it. She warmed up the same stew they had had the night before and ate a small meal for lunch, and when he had not returned before supper time, she knew that she was once again alone. This time, however, it seemed much harder to stand.

She ate supper without really thinking about what she was doing; her mind was on Brad and his question. She tended to Ty and Mary and took in enough wood from the barn to take her through the night. She sat in only the light that the fire gave off and began to cry. She wasn't sure just why really, but come the tears did. She cried for a long time. Eventually, long into the night, sleep came.

When she awoke, she heard a distant noise. Thinking she was still in some part of a dream she rolled over and tried to go back to her dream. No, she thought, this was not a dream it was……she listened harder, and yes it was BELLS.

"What on earth?" she said as she sprang from the bed. She went to the door and looked out onto the path. She heard the bells stop, and then all at once, Brad leapt down into the path, a big smile on his face.

"Miss me?" he said in a teasing way.

"Where have you been? Do you know how concerned I was?"

"Were you? Were you really worried about me?" he asked, looking deeply into her eyes. "Oh, I almost forgot, come on down. Do you need some help?"

A voice came from above them. She knew the voice but was unable to place it. Just about that time, a smiling face appeared above. It was Pastor Tolle. "I will be down there in a jiffy," said the pastor making his way slowly down the side of the pathway. Once on the ground, he looked up at Judy with a smile beaming from ear to ear. "Lucky for you my dear this old sleigh was in good enough shape to be used, and what better reason to get to use it than a wedding!"

Judy looked from Pastor Tolle to Brad, and then back again.

"Now Judy, I know you haven't given me an answer yet, and I don't mean to…well…rush you or anything, but I am not going to leave you alone for two or three weeks out here alone while this snow melts, and I am pretty sure that if we are going to be living together for almost a month that, well, in order to be proper and keep the shop keeper from gossiping about us, we need to make this official and get married right away. Wouldn't you agree?"

The absurdity of the whole thing caught up to her, and all she could do was begin to laugh. She kept laughing, and soon all three of them were laughing together. Brad finally looked at her and said, "Well what ya say Judy, wanna get hitched?"
She threw her arms around his neck and kissed him.

"Well, I will take that as a YES!" said Pastor, "Shall we take this wedding inside. I would like to get my sleigh home before dark."

The pastor performed a simple, but legal marriage ceremony as Mary looked on. Mary even voiced her opinion a time or two and made the three of them burst out in laughter. Once the "I do's" were exchanged, Pastor had a bite to eat and then prepared to leave. Brad helped him to gain access to the sleigh at the top of the snowbank.

As she heard the sleigh leave, Brad said, "Hey watch your head!" With that, a bundle came thundering down from the top, followed quickly by Brad.
She looked at the bundle and asked, "What's all that?"

"Presents!" he said, "Wedding presents."

He picked up the bundle, and they went into the house out of the cold. It still was surreal. She was a married woman. She was a Thompkins. She hoped her father knew from heaven what had really happened and forgave her for finally trusting one of the Thompkins enough to BE a Thompkins.

Brad put the bundle on the table, and stood between her and the bundle and said, "No peeking," as he began to untie the strings holding it together. "I was right about those furs." he said, "They brought a really good price in town, so I thought I would get a few things for you while I was in town."

He whirled around holding a brand-new winter coat. Such a grand coat it was too! It was long and wool and would surely be much warmer than the one her mother had been wearing for oh so many years. She tried it on, and it fit perfectly.

"Wait there is more." He said turning back around.

This time he came out with a piece of paper. He handed it to her, and she gave him a puzzled look. Then she began to read it. He had handed her the deed to the land. Her father's land. It had been registered in Brad and Judy Thompkins' names. He wasn't lying. He had told the truth and brought this to prove it. She began to feel tears coming to her eyes, but before she could say a word he turned back to the sack and said, "Just one more thing."

He then reached into the bag and took something out. It was small and he held it in his closed hand. He took her left hand and slipped a shiny gold band on her ring finger "I am sorry it's not a might fancier, this was all they had at the store in town. If you don't like it, we can get another one when we go into the big city come cattle selling time."

The tears of sheer joy rolled down her face, as she hugged him, and whispered "It's perfect. It's just what I want."

They were married. They would spend the rest of their lives together. As if in approval, Mary bleated from the corner, and they both laughed. They were ready to begin their lives together now.

Chapter 14

The winter seemed to pass by all too quickly for Judy. She still wasn't used to the fact she was not only a married woman, but her husband was the owner of a considerable chunk of property and livestock. He said his hired hands would take care of all his holdings over the winter months, so they stayed hunkered down at the Fern farm.

Judy liked married life. Brad was a good man. She had judged him and his family so unfairly. She prayed that God would break the news gently to her father, so he would understand that it was what was meant to be. Her mother, Judy knew, would understand. She had always liked Brad and had often remarked that he would make someone a good husband "someday." He helped her with all the chores, and together they had made only two trips into town all winter. One just before Christmas and one shortly after the big storm had passed.

Brad got Judy a buckling goat for Christmas. He said that Judy should start a small herd of milking goats, and Mary and Joseph, as the billy goat came to be known, would be the beginnings of her heard. Mary was a might upset at being banished back to the barn, but quickly warmed up to Joseph once she got over the new of him.

That Christmas was so special to Judy. Together they picked out their tree, brought it home, and decorated it with popcorn and homemade ornaments. Brad had carved a little heart and put the date they were married on it and placed it at the top of the tree. She had tried to make him a scarf. She was trying to teach herself from only her memories of what she had seen her mother do for so many years. The scarf was quite a sight. Holes where there shouldn't be, and not at all even like those her mother had always created, but Brad seemed pleased with her efforts and wore it proudly.

He even taught her how to make his trail biscuits. They were lighter and fluffier than any her mother used to make. Her mothers were good, don't think they weren't, but his were just, well, better. He had killed a goose near the pond, and they cooked the goose for their Christmas dinner. It was good to have a man in the house again. Her man, she thought. *MY MAN!* She did love him. How could she have ever managed before he came into her life? She even confessed that she called him Brat instead of Brad. He laughed hard and long, and he allowed that she and she alone, could call him that from now on!

She was happy there with him all winter long. They did everything together, but when the winter began to fade into spring, he let her know he would have to leave for a while to tend his herds. His hired hands had been tending things all winter, but they needed his long-overdue guidance, and he had to go for a few weeks out on the range. She told him she would be fine. She had survived before he came, and now that they were married, she was a fairly well to do woman. She would be just fine she assured him. Deep down, her heart sank to her toes. How could she manage without him after having had him to rely on? She wouldn't let it show to him, however. He needed her to be the self-reliant woman he first admired. She would be that even if she didn't really feel it. She would be a fearless rock. She knew that when he couldn't be there for her, she had what it took to survive.

The day he was to leave found the sun shining brightly. There were only a couple of inches of snow left on the ground and the spring air, although still chilled, held out the great promise of things to come. He offered for her to stay at his family home closer to town, but she wanted to stay where she was comfortable and that was the Fern Farm. He lingered a long time before he rode away from his bride. He looked back at her slight frame growing smaller as the distance grew greater. How could he leave her? How could he spend all that time away from her? He knew she would be fine. She was tough. She was capable. She was his. "Lord," he prayed aloud, "Be with my Judy while I cannot be. Protect her and keep her till I can come home to her again." Having left her in the capable hands of the Master, Brad turned toward the open road, and his duties. His bride would be here when he returned. This he knew.

Judy watched him ride away. She went back into the cabin and prayed for his safety and quick return to her. Then she began her day. She would do something special for him while he was away. She would make him a shirt. She had been working on her sewing all winter, and she was getting pretty good at it. She grabbed her coat and decided to walk to town for some new fabric. He would be so pleased when he returned to the presents! Yes, she thought she would surprise him with a new shirt, and it would give her something to do evenings beside the fire while he was gone.

When she got to town, everyone smiled and waved to her. They all shouted, "Morning Mrs. Thompkins," with a broad smile on their faces. This was the only the third time she had been called by her "new" name, and each time made her smile grow bigger. Mrs. Pringle almost met her at the door and allowed as to how good it was to see her in town again.

"What can I do for one of towns most important ladies?" gushed Mrs. Pringle. "Did you walk into town alone today? I did see your handsome husband leaving town this morning. How long will he be gone? I bet he is out doing what all the young men have been doing lately, fixing fences, branding calves, all the usual spring things."

By the time that Mrs. Pringle took a breath, Judy had already wandered over to the fabric section and was sorting through all the work shirt material. She half-listened to Mrs. Pringle as she went on and on asking, then answering her own questions. Soon, Judy had chosen a sturdy gabardine and handed it to Mrs. Pringle. Handing her the fabric didn't slow the shopkeeper's steady chatter one bit.

Judy spoke over her and said, "Two yards please and thread to match."

Mrs. Pringle measured out the fabric and got the thread. Judy browsed a bit and then came to the counter. She took out her little change pouch and asked what she owed.

"OH NO!" Mrs. Pringle protested, "Your husband told me that anything you needed to just put it on his tab. I promised that anything you wanted would go right to the tab. He is so good at paying his bills. No problem at all. I will just bag this up, and …Oh, would you like it delivered out your way later today?"

Judy was completely taken aback. Why this person had NEVER treated her with such respect and complete and total helpfulness? "Noo, no that's fine Mrs. Pringle, I will just take it with me. Thank you though."

She was in shock as she walked from the store. Wow, that was really strange! She knew Brad and his family had always been a big name in town, but she didn't know how big. Why, for some reason, being married to Brad made her some sort of royalty here. She shook her head in bewilderment and started down the street toward the end of town.

While she walked, she looked in the shop windows and saw the town's Sheriff rocking in his chair outside of the town hall. Sheriff was mostly an honorary title out here, as little criminal ever happened, but he was a good source of information for what was going on around the area. She passed pleasantries with him and then asked if a new doctor had been brought to town this winter. No doctor had yet been retained for the area, which meant the closest doctor was a day's ride away. Luckily, no major illnesses or injuries had occurred that the local livery owner couldn't tend to. He was used to setting bones and treating infections in animals, and in a pinch, he usually had an idea of what could be done for a person too. The Sheriff said he would be out to check up on her in a week, or so, as he had to ride out and take some personal property that belonged to old man MacDonald. His family in the east wanted a few things sent to them, and then the rest would be auctioned off later this year.

Judy asked him to join her for lunch that day, and he said that would be nice. They parted with him saying "You take care now, Mrs. Thompkins. See you soon."

Judy headed home. How her life had changed. She went from obscurity to some form of celebrity. She was not comfortable with this new distinction. It was easier to just blend into the woodwork. This would take some getting used to.

Chapter 15

Days passed by slowly for Judy. She enjoyed the luncheon with the Sheriff as it took her mind off the loneliness of the cabin. Mary was a bit preoccupied with Joseph most days, or perhaps it was the other way around. Either way, she didn't pay too much attention to Judy of late. It had been about three weeks since Brad had left. She missed him terribly, but she was doing just fine as far as the work on the farm went. The new shirt she was making was going well, and she expected that, although it was taking her WAY too long, it would be a nice gift for him when he returned. She expected him to come home soon and spent her free time watching the road for riders.

She awoke one morning quite ill. She figured that she had kept the stew a day longer than she should have and dumped out the rest of it later that morning. The sickness passed as the day went on, and she didn't give it another thought. However, when that queasiness continued every morning for three days, Judy was sure she had seen this illness before. Yes, about two years ago, in her mother when she was…when she was…. "Oh Lord," Judy said, "I am pregnant?"

Judy could only guess. She had no other women that she was close to ask about it, there was no doctor in town, so for Judy, it was a simple matter of ruling out other possibilities. When all else had been eliminated, she realized she would soon have Brat's baby. She laughed, a baby Brat! What would he say? She knew in her heart he would be pleased. He wanted a family. He wanted a big family. What would this mean for her and Brad?

She finished the shirt she was making for Brad. It looked really good, except one arm was just a mite longer than the other, but no one would ever notice that. Once that was finished, she took all the scraps of material that were in the sewing box and began piecing together a quilt for their baby. This would be a special gift for her baby. There were pieces of her father's flannel shirt and mother's old coat, some of the material from the shirt she made for Brad, some of her own dresses. She also used a small part of a christening gown belonging to her baby brother, and even a swatch from a handkerchief belonging to Brad's father. When it was finished, her baby would have all of those who love him or her most wrapping them in warmth and comfort.

She kept running through in her mind all the different ways she could tell him. Should she just come right out and say it? Should she hint and see if he catches on? Should she come up with some clever gift that would tell him, like baby booties? She simply couldn't decide on what she would do. In the meantime, she went about her daily routine of milking Mary and getting things planted in the garden.

They would have to do without milk for a while because it appeared that Judy was not the only one expecting. Judy would slowly dry Mary off and let her body work on baby-making and not milk production. What fun! Soon there will be babies everywhere! Brad even mentioned he might bring a calf home when he came. It would be nice to have more livestock. The hens had already hatched out six chicks this spring and were sitting on more eggs. She wouldn't let Judy gather them. She was adamant those were HER eggs, and she was keeping them. Judy didn't have the heart to push the issue, so she left those few eggs to her to hatch.

At night, Judy worked on her sewing and spent time in the good book. She waited, as patiently as possible, for her husband's return. *He should have been here by now.* she thought at the end of the fourth week. She told herself he had just needed more time to accomplish all he needed to do, and he would be home as soon as he could. She missed his presence so much. Just the sound of him breathing, in the still of the night, quieted her soul. God had truly sent him to her. She made a habit of thanking God daily for all His blessings. Her Brat always topped the list.

The weather got warmer, and Judy's morning sickness got less and less. She still wasn't showing but knew she would need to let out a couple of her dresses soon. The Sheriff had stopped a day or two ago to say he had word that Brad and his hands had been delayed due to some bear attacks on the cattle. They had to secure the herd and try to dispatch the offending bear before they could come home. Judy knew it was likely something like that which kept her beloved husband away so long. It was good of him to make sure she knew what was happening. He was so thoughtful that way.

If Judy knew where they were she would hire a horse and go out for a day, but that would likely be a bad idea, given her condition. She wasn't a frail woman, but she also knew that pregnancy needed to be treated gently. Lord knows how important this child was to her. It was a complete gift from God. She anxiously waited for the moment when she could tell her husband all about it.

Spring planting had begun with the peas and the heartier plants, and already they were starting to start up from the ground. She worked adding more and more seeds as the days grew warmer. She still had no more word from Brad but knew he would come home to her as soon as he could. Her sewing and knitting were improving with each project she began and finished. She was getting faster at them too. She would spend hours in the evening on her projects. She was tired of being alone, however.

One such night, she was sitting working on a knitting project when she heard a horse whinny. The noise caught her off guard. It had been so long since she had heard any noise from a horse on the farm. Shortly following the horse whinny, Mary began to bellow. Oh dear, she thought someone is in the barn. Before she could even rise from her chair, the door burst open, and there, standing in the doorway, was a short dirty man who she didn't know.

Chapter 16

The man stood in the doorway. His clothes were dirty, and his hair hadn't been washed in some time. He had been riding for a long time apparently, and Judy could hear his horse just this side of the barn breathing heavily.

"Well Missy," the man started, "I need a little hospitality from you today. You see?" He began to walk into the house and close the door, "I have been riding for a while now, and I see your light from a distance see, and I am needing of some food and a bit of rest, and I figured that someone as lucky as yourself to be here, all alone, with this big old cabin here, would be most grateful for some company. I just knew generosity would be common-like with someone as fortunate as you."

Judy's heart rose up to her throat. Who was this man? What was he doing here? She was truly frightened. She glanced at the shotgun in the corner. Brad had left it in case she had any trouble with coons or the like, but it was way out of reach to her now. She stared at the man, unable to move.

"Now Missy, you just get yourself busy getting me some of that fine stew you have there in that pot, while I take this here shotgun out to the barn with me while I water my horse. Now get busy, I will be back in just a few minutes, and I expect to have some of that fine stew I smell over there on that table when I get back here." With that statement, the man shuffled over to the corner where he had seen her eyes glance and picked up the loaded shotgun. His gait told her he had indeed been riding for a long time. He gave her a look that chilled her to the bone, and before he exited the house toward the barn, he said, "I will just put this old thing out in the barn.

After all, we wouldn't want it going off unexpectedly and getting someone hurt, now, would we?"

She thought about running, but she would never get by him between the barn and the house. There was no back door. *Why was there no back door?* she thought. She swung the stew back over the fire while she thought of what to do next. Her mind raced, but every idea she came up with seemed to be a non-productive one.

Before she could come up with a plan, the man came back through the door. "Good!" he said when he saw her at the fireplace, "Is that stew good and hot? I like my stew good and hot now!"

She said nothing but plated some stew and slid it to him as he sat at the table. He smiled and his smile revealed blackened and broken teeth. The sight of him sickened her. She quickly turned away. "Lord," she prayed silently, "Help me! Protect me from this stranger! I am frightened Lord, tell me what to do. But above all God, protect my baby."

He ate quickly then leaned back and pushed the plate away. "No biscuits?" he said and laughed at something that must have been funny only to him. He rose slowly, all the while, looking at Judy.

He walked to the fireplace, which caused Judy to take several steps away from it. She bumped into the rocker and quickly skirted her way around the chair.

"Where ya going, Missy?" he stated with his ragged smile, "I ain't gonna hurt ya! Much." With that, he lurched toward her.

Judy reacted without thinking and slapped his face HARD. She drew in a breath and held it waiting to see what he would do next. She had nowhere to run, nowhere to hide, and tears began to roll down her face.

He brought his hand up to his face rubbing the spot where her hand had landed and smiled with those black broken teeth. "Ok." he said, "I see how things are going to be. Yes, I see now." he said with a low menacing tone.

He grabbed her roughly and pulled her to him. She screamed without even realizing she was screaming. He laughed and wrapped his arms around her and held her close. Judy could smell him. He smelled of dirt, horse, and weeks of unwashed body. She was sickened by him and struggled to get away from him. He leaned his face into hers and she could feel his breath hot on her cheek. He was trying to kiss her!

"Lord," she cried out loud, "Where are you?" She screamed again as he tried to force her to kiss him. When he put his mouth to hers, she screamed again.

Judy had no choice but to be kissed by this disgusting man. He loosed one of her hands so he could grab her by her hair. With her hand now free her eyes wildly darted back and forth for some possible help. Then her eyes came to rest on the chair she had almost tripped over. *YES*, she thought if she could just get a little closer. She took a step toward the chair on unsteady feet. He pushed back into her, and she finally reached her desired goal.......

Chapter 17

Brad was tired. The last few weeks had been long and hard. He missed his new bride, but this was their future. He had to stay till the job was finished. The cattle had broken through many of the fences in the big snow this winter, and it was his job along with his hired hands to fix all those fences, find and regain their branded cattle no matter where they were, and also their potential calves. This was taking WAY longer than he had planned. He had to send one of his hands into a town in a few days for supplies, so he would send the letter he was composing for Judy with him so that she would know what was keeping him.

He took out the paper and pencil and began to write but had very hard time writing. He didn't want to write to her. He wanted to hold her in his arms. He wanted her beautiful lips on his. He wanted to watch her when she gently talked to that foolish goat of hers. She was more than life to him, and he was only half of himself without her near. *Maybe,* he thought, *if I go get the supplies I could swing by and at least see her.* Maybe he could spend one night there with her at the cabin. He knew that was not an option for him. He had to be here. These were good men, but they lacked focus and direction without him. This was a big job. They were not used to having all this to focus on. They were just cow hands, after all. They only knew hard work; they were not hired for their ability to make the hard decisions. That was what being the "boss" was about. Making sacrifices to do what needs to get done. He looked at the paper.

"My darling Judy," he began, "The work out here on the range is taking me longer than expected, my dear. I promise you that I will return as soon as I can. It may be another month, maybe even two, before I can return to you at the rate, we are recovering the cattle lost during the storm. This is our future, dear, and I have to tend to it. I would rather be with you doing anything as long as you were at my side, but for now, we cannot be together, my love. Rest assured my thoughts are with you daily and I will return to you as soon as I am able. In the meantime, my darlings, stay well, be safe, and think of me as much as I think of you. When I return, we will spend a few months working on making your home OUR home. We can add on, rebuild, whatever your heart desires. As long as you are happy, I will be happy. Anywhere I am with you I am home." He signed the note, "yours forever, Brat."

    He rolled it up and tied it with a slice of rawhide string. In the morning he would give this to Leon and give him the list of supplies in town. They were low on everything now and by the time he made the long journey to town and back again they would be likely out of most things. These were good men, but they got mighty mean when we run out of coffee! At least she would know when she read his letter that he missed her, he loved her, and he would return to her. He blew out the lamp and laid back on his bedroll. Most of the men were outside but Brad had the luxury of his own tent. Guess that was one of the perks of being the boss. No one could see how miserable he was without his beautiful wife, Judy. He pictured her snuggled in their bed quietly sleeping under the quilts. Her face highlighted by the flickering firelight was one of the most beautiful sights he had ever seen. He carried that vision with him now, but for some reason tonight it did not give him peace as it usually did. For some reason he was unsettled. He prayed to God to be with her tonight and every night, but for some reason, he prayed that he be with her, especially tonight. She needed God tonight he felt. He knew God would be there for her as he had always been. But tonight, especially, he knew she needed God or her husband, and since he couldn't be there, He would have to be.

Judy reached her hand down and felt near the chair. Finally, her hand landed on its desired target. She clasped her hand around it and raised her arm. He was putting his hands on her shoulders now, tearing at her dress. She prayed for her aim to be good.

She used all the strength she had in her and killed him with the sharpened wooden knitting needle. She turned and ran from the house. Leaving the door standing wide open she just kept running. It was a cool night, and she had no coat or shoes, but she couldn't feel the cold. She ran, just ran as fast as she could. She wasn't sure why or where she was running but she had to get away from him and the sight of what she had done to him.

She kept running until she got to town. She pounded on the home of the Sheriff. When he finally came to the door, she collapsed on him, and the world went black.

Chapter 18

When Leon Neal got to town it didn't take him long to discover from the lady shopkeeper that something terrible had happened in the little town. He left her with the list of goods to be purchased and headed to the Sheriff's office to get the low down on what was really going on. Leon had been with the boss for 5 years now. He knew him really well and knew how much his new little lady meant to him. If what he was hearing was true, he needed to let the boss know. But no sense getting him all riled up for nothing, best to get the whole story first.

Leon found that everyone he passed was talking about the same thing. The attack of the woman was big news. Not everyone knew who it was, nor what the outcome was, but everyone was talking about nothing else. This was BIG news. Nothing like this ever happened around this small town.

When Leon got to the Sheriff's office there was a note which read, "Out of town till after Lunch. See Judge Marcus while I am away." Leon didn't know the Judge, but he knew his offices were in the same building. This small town didn't really warrant a judge, but the judge liked it here and decided to stay about ten years back when he had visited here on a district court run. So, this became his base courtroom and he traveled from here when he needed to. Leon approached the official-looking door and knocked softly.

A gruff voice said, "Well, open the door and come in for goodness sake."

As Leon opened the door, he saw the face of the judge sitting pensively at his desk. A pile of papers sat in front of him, and he tapped a pencil on the papers like it might help him to figure out what he was thinking about.

"Judge Marcus, I don't know if you remember me, but..."

"Yes, yes, I remember you, Leon Neal," the Judge said hurriedly. "Say do you still work for Thompkins? You do, don't you?"

"Yes sir, I do. That's why I am here. I was sent to get supplies and heard there had been an attack and that it might be the new Mrs. Thompkins'. Is it true, Judge? Is she ok? What should I do?"

The judge went on to say that it was true. The newly married Thompkins' woman had been attacked by a drifter just last night. She had killed him. She was at the Thompkins' estate just outside town with some of the ladies from town caring for her. She was not well he told the hired hand. She had come miles barefoot and half-dressed into town for help. She was awake but running a high temp now. The judge suggested that Leon stop by the estate after getting his supplies to get an update on her condition. The town Sheriff and the constables were out taking care of the body of the drifter and helping to secure that area. They would look to see if there were any other drifters near abouts before coming back into town.

Leon couldn't believe his ears. It was true. Judy Thompkins had been attacked. She had been forced to kill a man to save herself. She did right, Leon thought, but now she was paying for her choice. As he drove the heavy-laden wagon up to the Thompkins' estate, called the Ample Acre Ranch, he saw two of the town's older ladies sitting on the porch. One had been working as a housekeeper for some time here at the ranch and the other he believed was the church piano player. He didn't know their names really, but knew they were trusted ladies who, no doubt, had offered to assist the new Mrs. Thompkins in her time of need.

"Ladies," Leon said as he got off the wagon. "I work for Mr. Thompkins. I hear his missus is not well. I have a letter for her, might she be able to receive me for a moment? "

The older of the two ladies got up and said she would see if she was awake. Leon waited on the ground next to the wagon. The other lady never took her eyes off him. No doubt the recent events had made all the local ladies a bit on edge.

When the lady came back, she told Leon that Judy was awake, but she was not a well woman. He could deliver his letter but then he must go. Leon agreed that he would not bother her any more than necessary to deliver his letter to her.

When Leon entered the room behind the older lady, he was instantly aware of how seriously ill this woman was. Her pale skin glowed with sweat and her cheeks were flushed with fever. She was awake but there was a distant look in her eyes that told him she was only just aware of his presence. The woman looked at him and told him again to hurry about his business, and then she directed him to a chair beside the bed and told Judy she would be just outside the door if she needed her. She shot a glance at Leon and left the room slowly, closing the door.

Leon took a seat in the chair and took a good look at this woman who was his boss' wife. He could see even through the fever that she was a beauty, and he could see why Mr. Thompkins didn't want to leave her. "Mrs. Thompkins my name is Leon Neal. I work for Mr. Thompkins. He sent me into town for supplies and I heard about what happened and wanted to pay my respects to you and deliver you the letter he sent with me for you."

Judy looked at the man. He was not familiar to her, but her heart told her he was a good man. "A letter?" she feebly said in a soft voice, "could you read it to me please."

Leon could read, but he wasn't really comfortable with reading a letter from a husband to his wife, but she was ill, and he felt as though somehow, he owed it to her after what she had been put through. He stuttered a few times over the tender nature of the letter that his boss had written. These types of words were never meant to be read by anyone but her, however, given the circumstances Leon guessed it would be ok.

When he finished the letter, he looked at her and her eyes were closed. At first, he thought she had fallen asleep and rose to leave, but she flew her eyes open and pleaded for him not to go yet.

"What did you say your name was again?" she asked.

"Leon, Leon Neal, Mrs. Thompkins"

"Leon, please I need you to help me. Will you help me, Leon?" Judy was almost begging this man she had only just met.

"Anything ma'am," Leon said, meaning every syllable.

"You have to promise me, Leon. Promise you will not tell my husband what has happened or that I am ill. He has work to do. I will be just fine. You must promise. Don't even mention that you saw me. Tell him you had the letter delivered and never left town. PLEASE, I am at your mercy, Mr. Neal. Please, do not tell my husband. There is nothing he can do. What's done is done and what will happen will happen no matter where he is. Let him do what he must with a peaceful heart." With that Judy had no more strength. She sank into the pillow and her eyes closed.

Leon was not about to let this wonder of a woman down. The boss had indeed chosen well. She was a lot like Brad Thompkins; brave, strong, selfless, dare he say, stubborn. Leon rose from the chair and put a hand on her arm. "I promise," he said quietly, and he left the room.

On the long wagon ride back to base camp he thought long and hard about his promise. It was wrong to keep news like this from the boss, but he HAD promised. A promise is a promise after all, and Leon wasn't about to break his word to this strong beautiful woman. No, he wouldn't tell, unless something made him tell. Leon Neal was a man of his word. He wouldn't tell.

Chapter 19

Judy spent several days in and out of a fevered state. Since there was no doctor in town the ladies who attended to her did what they could to help the young Mrs. Thompkins recover. They boiled willow barks and made tea to help with the fever. They provided her with cool compresses and even had some ice brought from the icehouse to help bring down her burning temperature, but in the end, all they could really do was wait out the illness and pray she would survive. The exhausting run through the cold night air with no shoes was too much for her body to take and she had come down ill by the next morning.

The ladies knew Judy's secret as they, having been with child before, knew the signs and saw her belly just beginning to show. They said prayers for the tiny life inside her, but they feared that if the child did survive, it might not be "right" given the mother's high fevers. That type of thing had happened before. They had seen children born of women who had suffered a similar illness be born with "problems". Deaf, blind, or simple-minded were among some of the things they had seen. All though any child was a gift from God, no one wanted to think their child wouldn't be born perfect.

When Judy's fever finally broke, she had been ill for eight days. She was weak but alive. Once she was fully aware of her surroundings, she immediately asked the ladies who were attending her about her baby. They assured her that her baby would be fine, both knowing full well that it might be a lie, but there was no sense telling this poor weak child that at this point. Perhaps when she was stronger, but they would not mention it now.

As the days went by and Judy grew stronger, she began to worry about her farm and animals there. She was assured that her goats were fine as they had been brought here and the hands were looking after them. Here, Judy had been told, was her husband's home. This place was like a palace to Judy. Real lace curtains on the windows, she lay in a store-bought bed with store-bought sheets, and there was a bureau with four drawers by the window and a lovely picture and basin for washing on top. There was even a really fancy ceramic chamber pot under the bed! She had never seen such things outside of the Sears and Roebuck catalog in the local store at Christmas time.

When she was well enough to get some fresh air, the ladies got her dressed in a pure white nightgown made of the softest material Judy had ever seen. They put a robe around her shoulders they said belonged to the former Mrs. Thompkins, Brad's mother. It was truly elegant, adorned with beautiful, embroidered flowers on the cuffs and collar, and made from silk all the way from Paris France. She felt like she was in some sort of fairy tale when she descended the stairs to the front door.

She had never seen the inside of the Thompkins home. Although she had suspected it was very opulent and grand, her imagination could not have done the real thing justice. Everywhere one looked was rich darkly stained woodwork. Not the bare logs like everyone usually had in a home, but real milled boards which Judy knew would have had to have been brought in from the bigger towns in the area as they didn't have anything but a small mill that didn't produce lumber this fine. There were chairs covered with the most lovely, patterned fabric that she thought it a shame to sit upon them. There was a sitting couch too, where two, or maybe even three, people could sit all at once. They were much richer than she had ever expected.

After the ladies had her in a comfortable rocker on the porch in the sun with a blanket over her legs, they left Judy to prepare some lunch for her. Judy surveyed the grounds of the ranch. There were two BIG barns, and she could see many horses grazing in the pasture. In a smaller pasture, she saw Mary and Joseph happily munching on bushes just over the fence. "The grass is always sweeter on the other side of the fence," Judy thought. The goats looked good, and Judy knew they had been getting good care.

Every time one of the workers about the farm walked by the front of the house, they would always tip their hat in a gesture of respect and say "Morning, Ma'am," or "Morning, Mrs. Thompkins." She realized, all at once, this whole place, the barns, the house, the livestock, the land, all of it belonged to her husband and therefore to her as well. "Lord, what did I do in my life to warrant such a grand blessing as my husband and all this? And now, Lord, to add a baby onto that! Why, I just can't express how truly grateful I am. Thank you for my life."

Judy felt a bit out of place here, but as the days went by and she grew stronger and felt her baby grow inside her she found she was falling in love with this beautiful home the Thompkins had. The hired hands were all wonderful people, and they were a bit confused when she offered to help with their duties, but graciously declined her offers of assistance. This type of life was strange to Judy, but Brad was used to it, she thought. He grew up here. This was HIS home. The home she had outside of town was little more than a memory of the tragedy. Thus, although she had originally wanted to stay there for the memory of what her father had built and the efforts, he had done to get them a home, she knew that Brad's home may be a more fitting place to raise a Thompkins' heir. She would ask Brad to build a nice little fence around the graves on the property and perhaps they could rent it to a young struggling family so that they may have a chance to buy it one day. It was a good home, just not for her anymore. She had to come to grips with the fact that Brad was born to live here, to raise his family here, and she was his wife and would be where he should be. Her mother told her that's what a good wife did. They followed their man no matter where that took them. God led the man of the house, and the man led the family. She would let go of the "in charge" woman she had been forced to be and let her husband be in charge. Once she realized this, she seemed more at peace than she had been in years.

Then her thoughts went to the other man. The man she had murdered. He was a bad man, and she was defending herself, but still, she took a life. That was not her life to take. How could she have done that? How could she have killed that man? God would surely rebuke her one day for taking the life of that man. She was as sure of that as she was sure she was blessed beyond her comprehension by her husband. She prayed silently for God to not make amends for the life she took by taking her child. Then she thought, *No! God is not a vengeful God.*" She was truly sorry for what she had done and perhaps God would forgive her given the circumstances. Perhaps......time would tell.

Chapter 20

The men had worked hard for many weeks on the range, and it was quickly coming to an end. Leon had kept his promise to Mrs. Thompkins. He had not told the boss about how ill his wife had been. He had, however, prayed that she had survived. The issue was gnawing at him the last few days and he felt led to tell the boss. They would all be leaving for home in a day or two anyway. He had done his job. He should be with his wife; Leon needed to let him know.

After breakfast, Leon motioned for Mr. Thompkins to step aside so that they might talk in private. Leon thought he had done well not to let on, but it was time.

Without a big fanfare, he told the boss that he needed to hear him out before he spoke. Then he went into the whole story of how his bride had begged him not to tell him, however, since his job was done, he figured his promise had been kept and now it was time for him to know what was happening.

Brad Thompkins stared at him for a moment, then turned on his heel, mounted his horse, and sped off in the direction of town. Leon knew, when he saw him again, he would likely collect his last pay and would no longer be employed by the Thompkins family. Leon had kept his word. To him, that was all that mattered. His word was his bond. Sometimes in life, a man's word is all he has, Leon felt proud even if he lost his job, and his integrity was intact.

As Brad drove his horse hard toward town, he had time to think about what he had been told. He knew it took a lot for Leon to have not told him, he respected that, but at the same time, he was furious that he didn't know his wife needed him. He would have killed the man who attacked her, but she had already taken care of that herself. God bless her. She never should have been put in a position to have to have done that. Why was he not there when she needed him most? All for a few cattle, what do they matter when it comes to family? NOTHING! "I am a fool, Lord. I am such a fool." he said out loud, "Forgive me, heavenly Father, for not taking care of my wife." There was no one to blame for this but himself. This was his entire fault.

When he rode fast past the Fern farmhouse, he wanted to stop, wanted to see where it had happened, but he needed to get to her. His beloved wife, my how he loved the sound of that, he had to get to her and see for himself he was ok. He had to talk to her. He had to apologize for not being there when she needed him. He had to make this up to her, somehow.

As he rode through town, the buildings and people were nothing more than a blur to him. He was single-minded and the only thing he could see was his destination and HER.

As the house came into view, he drove the horse harder. He knew he was being really hard on his horse, but at that moment that was the last thing he was worried about. When the porch came into view, he had hoped she would be there, resting after her illness and ordeal. She was not there. Where was she? He brought the horse up to a sliding stop in front of the house. He flew up the stairs and crashed through the door. As he stepped through the threshold of the home, he found he was already yelling her name.

"JUDY!" He called again and again, but no answer came.

As he was about to run upstairs and search each room, the housekeeper emerged from the kitchen. "Now, now settle down young man, your Mrs. is fine." She said with a smile.

"Where is she?" he said breathlessly, "Where can I find her?"

"She is in the barn where she always is, with that foolish goat of hers." the housekeeper huffed.

With that, Brad turned and started for the door. He jumped off the porch and as he started toward the barn, he saw Judy just exiting the barn door. He ran to her. She saw him and met him halfway. He swept her into his arms and held her close. She threw both arms around his neck and hugged him tightly. He whispered "I am so sorry" over and over again in her ear. After a considerable amount of time passed, he put her on the ground. It was then that he saw what his eyes had not noticed.

He placed his hand on her ever so slightly swollen belly and looked her in the eye with a questioning look.

"Yes," she said, "about 4 months." Judy smiled at her husband and together they shared a moment of awe that can only come from knowing that together they had made a precious life.

He carried her to the porch despite her pleas to put her down. She relished the attention he was paying her. She had missed him more than she ever realized. He set her down on one of the rockers and pulled the other one close in front of her.

Slowly over the better part of two hours, she revealed to him what had happened in his absence. She cried when she told him about killing the man, but he told her she had no choice. He asked about her illness and why she had not sent for him. She, being the stubborn beautiful girl, he had always known, told him that there was no need to bother him with a simple illness.

After a bit of scolding, she finally promised to never do that again. When all the details were revealed, he spent several minutes just staring into her eyes. Somehow, they were different. Somehow, the same beautiful eyes seemed deeper and darker. She had been through something that had really shaken her. She had taken a man's life and Brad knew that changes a person. She was changed. He wasn't sure if it would be a good or a bad change, but she had surely changed. Her eyes were unlike he had ever seen before, colder, harder somehow.

The housekeeper caught Brad's eye and motioned secretly for him to come in for a minute. He told Judy he needed something to drink, and he would get them some lemonade. She offered to get it. "OH NO! You and my child sit right there Mrs. Thompkins!"

When Brad entered the house, the housekeeper motioned for him to be quiet while they walked to the other side of the house and into the kitchen. While she got a couple of glasses of cool lemonade ready for the couple she hesitantly began to speak.

"Brad, my darling boy, I don't wish for your missus. To hear me. I don't want to upset her, Poor thing. Lord knows she has been through WAY too much in her short life, but there is something you need to know."

Brad had known this woman all his life. She was like a second mother to him, and he had rarely seen her with a look of such concern. "What's wrong?" he asked, "Is she ok? Is there something else going on?"

"She will be fine dear, but…well…. There is something you need to know. It's the baby."

Before she could say another word, Brad said, "Is there something wrong with our baby?"

"Well now this is just the thing, your little Mrs. was sick Brad, very sick. She had a very high fever for quite a few days. We did all we could to get her temperature down, but, well, a fever like that isn't good for a baby growing inside. It is possible that something might not be right. She was burning hot for so many days. We don't know for sure if it hurt the baby, but it could, it might have. You need to be prepared. It's possible that your baby may not be perfect. I don't want to scare you, but you should know. With a fever like that, it's possible there might be something …well …. not right." She stopped talking and looked at him.

This news caught him off guard and he found himself bracing his weight on the table. In the last 9 hours, he had found out his wife had been attacked, killed to protect herself, had fallen ill, recovered, and that he was to be a father, and now he was being told that his baby may be damaged somehow? What was a man to say to news like this?

"Now Brad, I am telling you this so at least one of you is prepared. Just in case. You may have a beautiful baby, sound, and whole, but it is possible, just possible, that it might not be. I know you're strong and can handle this news, but if I were you, I wouldn't tell your little lady. She has been through enough poor thing."

Brad grabbed the glasses of cool drinks. He turned, took a deep breath, plastered a smile on his face, and returned to the porch.

She was beautiful sitting there. More beautiful than she had ever been, she carried his child.

"Does the town have a doctor?" Brad asked.

"No, not yet why?" she innocently said watching the goats playing in the paddock with a smile.

"My wife and baby need to be seen by a doctor. You have been ill and tomorrow I will take you into the 'big city,' "he said with a laugh," and we will make sure you and that baby are just fine."

"Don't be silly, "Judy quipped, "I am fine, and this baby is fine, but if it will make you happy, I will go in to see the doctor with you tomorrow." She smiled a devious smile that she used when she was humoring him.

"Good, it will make me happy. We will pack lunch and have a picnic on the way home at the bridge. It's lovely there and we can get caught up on some missed time. My how I have missed you." With that, he kissed her gently on the cheek and sat beside her to sip his drink and think about all he had learned today. Tomorrow, he would hopefully get some fears alleviated. Tomorrow will be a better day.

Chapter 21

The next day found the sun shining early. A lovely picnic lunch was prepared, and Brad loaded that and a few other items into the buckboard, and they struck out for the three-hour trip to Casper. This was an up-and-coming city, and Brad wired ahead to their best doctor that they would be in today and why. The journey was long and bumpy and, although they made a couple of rest stops, they made a decent time and were entering the bustling small city. This was not like the town they were used to. In their town, everyone knew everyone else. Here, there were people everywhere, coming and going and sitting and standing. There were cattlemen, ladies in fancy dress, men in suits, and some ladies who, judging by their attire, had less than stellar reputations. Brad quickly looked away from the scantily clad women in time for his wife to give him a scowl. "What?" he asked with a smirk.

Judy shook her head. He was teasing her she knew, but still…how did these women dare be caught in public with hardly a thing covering their, well, EVERYTHING!? What would her father have thought of THAT? Or Pastor? She was not sure the city was a fitting place to be but knew her husband wanted to err on the side of caution where their child was concerned. He was so happy about this new life inside her. *How wonderful!* she thought, *and what a divine father he would be.* She silently prayed for a little boy just like his daddy, but a little girl would be good too. When she had asked Brad what he wanted all she could get him to say was a baby. That just frustrated her. She didn't want that answer; she wanted to know if he wanted a boy or girl. But all he kept saying was baby…beautiful healthy baby. Sometimes he can be so exasperating. She wondered if her mother ever got frustrated with her father like this. Then she laughed and said to herself.... yes, I am sure all women do. Men are just that way. Brad asked what she was chuckling about, but she ignored the question.

When they got to the building where the doctor's office was there was a rather large sign hanging on the front which said Dr. Thomas Leavy, M.D. General Medical Care, Surgeon, Dentistry, Eyeglasses, Certified Vet. Brad got his little bride down carefully from the buckboard. He had begun treating her like a fine piece of china. She absent-mindedly swatted his arm when he held on to her a second too long to make sure she was "stable" on the ground. He let go and she began to go up the stairs to the door to the doctor's office. Brad hurried and caught up to her and opened the door before she could get to it. "I am not a china doll Mr. Thompkins," she said.

He smiled warmly down at her and said in a hushed tone, "You're my china doll."

Judy couldn't help but smile. He had so much love in his eyes that it almost made her want to cry.

They approached the desk where a nurse in a white dress and hat worked on paperwork at a desk. They waited for a few moments until she finished her writing and looked up from her work. "Yes, can I help you?" she said a bit drily.

"I wired the doctor yesterday, I am Brad Thompkins, and this is my wife, Judy. He knows we are coming."

"Oh yes, Mr. and Mrs. Thompkins. We have been expecting you. We have several tests and examinations for your wife. It will take a while; you can wait out here in the waiting room or perhaps get a bite to eat and come back."

The nurse was pleasant enough but rather abrupt in her manner. Judy suspected it was from years of dealing with this busy office. She whisked Judy off and into a small office exam room. She left her alone for about 10 minutes and the doctor came in reading a chart.

"Mrs. Thompkins, I just spoke to your husband, and he told me about your ordeal and recent illness. I think he was wise to have us take a look to make sure you and your baby are fine."

"Doctor," Judy said," I don't mean to be impertinent, but I am feeling fine after my illness, a bit weak perhaps but fine. The man who assaulted me is dead and therefore I have put that incident behind me. I frankly don't see the need to waste money on a doctor if I am feeling well."

The doctor smirked a bit then sat on the edge of his desk, looked Judy in the eye, and said, "Your husband warned me you are a stubborn headstrong girl! HA, guess he was right! Look, Mrs. Thompkins, I won't examine you if you don't want, but frankly, I share your husband's concern. You were very ill, with a high fever, that horrible incident was a shock to your system and therefore to your baby. There is reason to suspect that there may be issues, now if you say no…."

Judy cut him off, "Are you saying there may be something wrong with my baby?"

"No, I am saying we should check and make sure there is nothing wrong with your baby. This little life depends on you my dear, we need to make sure with all you have been through that things look… well…. right." the doctor said rather matter of factly.

Judy agreed with that logic. This little life was now her first priority. Making sure this baby was ok was important. Brad hadn't been overreacting. She wished she had her mother here to talk to, to ask questions to. Judy had a million questions that she had no one to talk to about. She felt as though she was once again in the blizzard. She couldn't see ahead of her and looking backward did no good. All she had to go by was what she had heard and witnessed when her mother had her little brother. This doctor perhaps was someone she might trust to ask the rather delicate questions of. After all, he was a doctor; he should know what she should expect. He should be able to tell her what was normal, what was not normal.

So, while the doctor and nurse went about doing the exam and running some tests that Judy didn't understand, she pestered him with a multitude of questions that she had been thinking of ever since she discovered she was pregnant. The doctor, and even occasionally the nurse, who warmed up a bit as you got to know her, dutifully answered all her questions.

When the doctor had completed his exams and tests, he called Brad into the room. Judy was sitting in one chair in front of the doctor's desk and Brad took the other chair and reassuringly grabbed Judy's hand.

"I will be right with you folks; I just have to talk to my nurse a moment." And with that, the doctor left the room.

Brad and Judy didn't speak a word while they waited. The air was tense waiting for what the doctor had to say. Brad kept squeezing her hand gently and looking around the room at all the highly technical medical equipment. He had no clue what most of them might be used for. If the truth be told he was a bit afraid to know about some of them.

When the doctor came back into the room, he was carrying a book with him, reading as he walked. He went behind the desk and Judy and Brad sat up in the chair in anticipation of what he would be telling them.

The doctor cleared his throat and looked up from his book and smiled. "Ok, let me tell you what we found." He turned to Judy and began again, "Judy, overall, you are a very healthy young woman, despite your recent illness. Although I didn't find anything amiss with the tests, I am a bit worried about your little one, however. Now, before you get all upset, let me explain what I mean."

Brad broke in and looked at Judy and said, "Darling, perhaps you should let the doctor and I talk. Would you like to rest in the waiting room for a bit?" Judy shot him a glance that said it all without saying a word. She did NOT wish to rest in the waiting room while he and the doctor discussed her baby.

The doctor put up his hand and said, "Mr. Thompkins, your wife is perhaps the strongest willed person I have ever had the pleasure to meet. She is quite capable of handling what I am about to say, I am sure of it."

Brad wasn't happy, but he was outnumbered.

The doctor continued. "Judy, may I call you Judy?" Judy nodded her head and he continued, "Your baby appears fine." Both Brad and Judy let a long breath out and smiled at each other before the doctor went on again. "However, that doesn't mean that it's going to be normal."

"Wait, you just said our baby was fine, now you say it's not? What are you trying to say?" Judy's tension and exasperation showed immediately.

"Ok Judy, hear me out. Because of your shock and the high temperatures, you suffered because of your illness, it is possible, not definite, but possible, that you may have some issues. I fully expect you to carry full term, and for that matter deliver normally, but science and all my knowledge and fancy tests can't tell us everything. God has the final say in these things. Babies born to women who have had high fevers or shocks less than what you have gone through have delivered babies with …issues. Some of the things that can possibly happen are blindness, malformed limbs, deaf, or mute, or nervous conditions, paralysis, and the list goes on. This is not to say that this is GOING to happen, however. As I said, "God has the final say.," but you two need to prepare yourself in case it happens. Now I can't tell you any more than that. It MIGHT happen, keep praying and asking for God to be with you. I will be adding you both to my prayer list as well."

Judy felt her eyes begin to tear up. She HATED it when she cried around others. Brad put his hand on her shoulder and said "Now Judy, our baby is going to be just perfect, and if, in God's infinite wisdom and mercy, it is not 100% the way it should be, we will not love him or her any less. Don't you fret now, God will decide what our baby will be and how we will proceed with this wonderful little gift He has given us. Trust that God knows what He is doing, and he would not give us anything unless he knew it was the right thing for us. He has us firmly in His hands. He protects us and keeps us in His loving arms. He will do no less for this beautiful life we created."

"I couldn't have said it better myself!" The doctor smiled and went to Judy to hand her a handkerchief. "Judy, any child you bear will be endowed with your strong will, your husband's kind loving heart, and God's grace…how can it be anything but perfect no matter what it may be like?"

The words from the men made her heart hurt a little less. She dried her tears and Brad and she rose to leave. Brad went to hand the doctor some money, but the doctor waved him off. "Wait for that Mr. Thompkins, I want to see your wife again in about 4 months, which should put her pretty close to delivery, perhaps we can tell more then. Let me see that will put us at….," and he flipped through a calendar, "October, shall we say the 10th?"

Brad looked at Judy who nodded her head and Brad also affirmed they would be back on the 10th of October.

As they rode back home, they spoke little, both mulling over the findings of the doctor. They stopped in a beautiful glen near the bridge and had a lunch of chicken and biscuits. Neither of them ate much, and before long they were back on the road. It was just about supper time when they made it back to the ranch. Judy told her husband she was going to rest a bit before supper and went to lie down. She thought about the words her husband spoke and wanted to take them to heart. Deep down she knew he was right, but another side of her deep down knew that if something was wrong with her baby, it was her fault. God would be showing her about her transgressions for taking a life that was not hers to take. Yes, she knew with all certainty that if her baby was not perfect, she would love it perhaps even more than a "normal" child, but she knew that for that child's life, she would look and see her mistakes, her shortcomings set upon her child. She got to her knees and prayed that He put the burden on her not her child for her mistakes, her failings. She knew God would hear, and she hoped He would show his mercy.

Brad sat on the porch and knew no matter what, this child was conceived in love and would be loved no matter if it was healthy or not. He already loved this tiny baby. How could he not….it was growing inside the woman he loved more than life itself. "God's will be done," he said out loud, and picked up his well-worn Bible and began to read.

Chapter 22

The months passed by, as summer months usually do. Lazy days spent tending gardens and enjoying the pleasures of living in the heart of God's most beautiful country. Judy's body grew and her husband teased her that she was going to fall over backward if she stuck her tummy out anymore. Judging from the information she had pried from the doctor, her pregnancy was progressing very normally. It was easy to forget about the possibility of anything being wrong. Judy had, with help from the sweet-natured housekeeper, learned to knit and had fashioned several warm outfits made out of soft yellow and green colors for her baby. Brad would sit and stare at her knitting the tiny things for the baby and just smile a warm smile at her. He had a beautiful room upstairs fashioned into a baby's room. He made a wonderful cradle and several other pieces of furniture to put in the room. When her baby came into this world it would be surrounded with love and wonderful joyous things that came from those who love him/her most.

The housekeeper had gone to the old cabin and gotten the quilt that Judy had made way back in the spring. Judy had yet to go back to the homestead. She simply couldn't face seeing where she had watched that man crumple to the ground. She was a strong woman, but she couldn't face that yet.

Brad had told her that he wanted them to live here now, given what had happened. She did not fight him on that. Her husband wanted only what he thought was best for her and the baby, and she knew that.

The summer brought joy to Judy's heart. Her beloved goat gave birth to a beautiful set of twins, one doe, and one buckling. The buckling was sold to a local family, and Joseph the herd sire…she joked that 3 goats were really not a herd yet…. but he was put in a neighboring pen while Mary raised her baby. The baby was called Daisy because Mary really stood for Marigold, and Judy wanted to stick with the whole flower theme. Brad let her do as she wished with her goats. They were hers after all.

He still treated her like she would break, but the few arguments they had were about him trying to take too much care of her. She had never given up her stubborn streak and insisted on tending the garden and doing what she could to contribute. When canning time came, she had to compromise and only work in the mornings as Brad was convinced, she was overdoing it. He was such a worrywart now. She hoped that once the baby was born, she would see that behavior let up on that a bit. Ever since he had returned from the range this spring, he had not left for more than two days at a time and when he did, he insisted that she stay right at the house where there were always people around.

Mary's baby was almost as big as Mary herself and fully weaned by the time October came. Mary gave more milk than ever and life on the farm for animals and humans alike was wonderful.

They attended church in town every Sunday and often had the pastor to dinner on Sundays as well. The pastor had been told what the doctor had told them. As the time came for them to return to see the doctor again, and Judy's time grew near the pastor asked the entire congregation to pray for the tiny child she carried and for its parents. No one prayed harder than Brad and Judy who prayed together nightly before bed.

Judy and Brad planned to stay overnight in Casper one night as the doctor wired him and asked if they could come in the afternoon on the 10th. Judy had never before been in a hotel and she was actually quite excited at the prospect.

How different her life had become. Brad told her they looked to make a good deal of money this fall when they sold off some of the cattle herd. He said he was going to buy their child a pony with a bit of the money. Judy just shook her head at him. He tried so hard to think of everything. He did a good job too.

They packed up the wagon with their luggage and some travel food and headed toward the big city of Casper. Her time was close now. Soon, they would know if God intended to make her pay the ultimate price for her sins. She had become more accepting of things no matter what the outcome. She would love this baby even if it was deformed ….it was her and Brad's. No matter what, this baby would be theirs.

Chapter 23

Brad looked at his wife. She was more beautiful than he had ever seen her. She was soon to give birth to a baby, his baby, and a complete gift from God. He wondered if it would be a boy or a girl. He didn't really care. Either would be wonderful as far as he was concerned. He could see a bit of distress in her face now and again and wondered if the bumpy road might be a bit too much for her being so close and all, but the doctor must have known what kind of a journey it would be before he told them to come. She cradled her belly like she was already holding that baby.

Town was a bit different this time of year. The air had a bit of a chill in the evening and the attire a bit more conservative given the season. Why even the scantily clad women had shawls and capes on. They had arrived in town a bit early for the appointment and Brad decided to take them on a little shopping trip. He had never really taken his bride into a real store other than the small mercantile they had at home. He stopped the wagon between the doctor's office and the beginning of a row of shops. These were not mercantile. These were fancy shops. Some displayed the latest fashion for the ladies, some had top hats and coats for a gentleman, and another one was nothing but toys for children and clothes for them. Judy walked with him arm in arm down the street, but the children's shop drew her attention as Brad suspected it would. He took her inside and saw Judy's eyes grow wide at all the wonderful, beautiful things a "well to do" child might indulge in. Judy set her eye on a hanging thing perched over a cradle. Brad didn't know what it was called, but it had delicate ceramic depictions of angels and clouds hanging on strings beneath a golden star. Judy delicately touched each piece and looked at Brad with wonder.

The clerk came over and said," It's the latest mobile design from Europe. Isn't it lovely? My …your baby would surely enjoy falling to sleep watching angels now, wouldn't they?"

Judy spoke first, "I am sure, but something this lovely is way beyond our means."

Brad scowled at her, "Now wait just a minute here, nothing is too good for OUR baby. How much is it, Miss?"

"Oh, it's actually quite reasonable sir, only $3.75. After all, it does come from Europe. " The salesclerk said.

"Box it up please; we will be back tomorrow before we leave to collect it," Brad said without hesitation. That was a tidy sum for a hanging thing, but Judy really admired it, and his child deserved the best.

Judy stared at him in astonishment. Why that was a ridiculous price, but at the same moment she was a bit giddy at the thought of hanging that over the beautiful crib Brad had made. Brad nodded his head to her as if to say, it's ok.

As soon as they left the store, Judy stopped and looked at him. "Are you mad? Why that is a week's wages for the hired hands, and for something so frivolous too."

Brad looked at her and calmly said, "Judy, consider it my gift to our baby. And that's the end of it."

Judy just stared at him but knew he meant business. She loved him so.

They got checked into their hotel room before going to their appointment. This hotel was the grandest thing Judy had ever seen, even grander than the ranch house. Red velvet chairs and couches in the lobby, real brass beds, and plush mattresses and pillows in the room. Why there was even a water closet in the hall? Brad had to show her how that worked as she had never even seen one before. She had heard tell of them, but never did she think she would actually see one, much less get to use it!

After they were settled into the room, they got a sandwich at the diner down the street and headed to their appointment. Brad had the hotel ask the livery to take care of the buckboard and horses for the night and as they approached the office, the livery was just collecting the wagon.

When they entered the office there was no one around, so they sat and waited a few minutes till the nurse came into the room.

"Ah Mrs. Thompkins, I was just setting up the exam room for your appointment. Won't you come with me please?"

Brad helped Judy to get out of her chair. She never thought just standing up would be so hard, but she was a bit heavy on the front these days. She followed the nurse to the exam room and before long the doctor came in. The exam was not the type of thing that one would talk about in a pleasant society, but Judy surmised it was part of being a doctor that made a ladies' body a clinical thing. At least that made it easier for her to reconcile with.

The doctor looked up from his exam to her and said, "Judy have you had any pain or cramping?"

Judy explained that she had a bit on the ride over but figured it was a bumpy ride and nothing to worry about, so she had dismissed it.

"My dear Mrs. Thompkins, you are close to delivery. I mean any time now. You won't be headed home until you have that baby. Those pains I suspect were early contractions. You are soon to be a mother." he said with a smile wider than she had ever seen on him. "And what's more," he said, "I can see no issues to worry about. Everything looks quite normal."

Judy was shocked and excited at the same time. She dressed hurriedly and joined Brad in the waiting room where the doctor was telling Brad what she already knew. He rushed to her, picked her up and hugged her, then thinking better of his actions, carefully put her down, and asked if she was ok. Judy and the doctor laughed at him. The doctor told them to stay in town for the next few days and to send for him if she went into labor no matter the hour. He also said that Judy should try to rest and take it easy as much as possible.

Brad escorted her to their hotel room, and then said he had to check on the horses and take care of a few things but would be back as soon as possible. He let the front desk know the delicate condition his wife was in, and they told him they would assist them in any way possible. He wired the ranch to let them know of the delay in coming home and went to the local bank to get a bank draft to cover expenses. He stopped by the diner and asked if it was possible to get his wife's meals delivered to the room since she was under doctor's orders to rest. They said it would not be a problem and would take care of everything. Before going to the hotel again he went back to the toy store and found a soft stuffed rabbit that he had seen in the shop. He purchased it and tucked it under his coat as he entered the room.

Judy was propped up on pillows reading the Old Testament on the bed when Brad came in. She always had trouble following all the begat this one and begat that one, so she often tried to reread it to try to clarify all that in her brain. He beamed at her, and she knew he was up to something. He pulled the stuffed rabbit from his coat and placed it on her tummy. She picked it up smiling, looked it all over, and said, "Brat you forgot to put a bullet hole in its head like the other ones you got me." They laughed.

The diner did as promised and brought dinner for them to the room at about 6:30 that evening. They had a lovely meal of stew, biscuits, and pickles. Those pickles tasted especially good to Judy, but she didn't know why as she wasn't a big fan of pickles normally. They talked about how their lives would soon change and all the wonderful plans they had for their baby. They both had hopes and dreams and wanted only the best for their children. Brad said this was only the first of many, and at this point, Judy was not sure just how many he was talking about. He allowed as to how the more the merrier and she told him that of course, he thought that way, HE didn't have to have them all, but she was only joking. She was so excited to bring this life into the world. They went to sleep lying in each other's arms, dreaming of the future and their child.

She awoke with sharp pain. The hour was late, very late. Brad slept peacefully beside her. She slid out of bed and went to sit in the chair. She threw a blanket over herself and settled in for what was likely to be a long evening. She had heard tell of women being in labor for hours and hours and surmised that was just how it was. She saw no need to wake Brad just yet. When her water broke on the way to the water closet, she got a bit frightened but had talked to enough ladies by this time to know that was also to be expected. She got cleaned up a bit and decided it was time to get Brad up. He was about to become a father.

Chapter 24

The doctor had been sent for immediately, and Brad got word they were to meet them at the office down the street. Brad wrapped a blanket around his wife and scooped her up before she could protest and carried her down the stairs and out into the street and started for the doctor's office despite her shouts of protest. When a contraction hit her, he could feel her body tense and could tell she was in a great deal of pain although she had yet to cry out. He kicked the bottom of the door, and a rather sleepy-eyed nurse opened the door. "This way." she said and walked them to a room Judy had never seen before. There were two beds there and Brad placed her gently on one of them. As another contraction wracked her body, the nurse said "Ok, Mr. Thompkins, time for you to wait outside. We have a baby to deliver." With that, she shoved him through the door and shut it.

The doctor came into the hall and told Brad, this might be a long night so he should just get comfortable, and he would be out to talk to him as soon as there was anything to tell.

Brad paced for what seemed like hours, inside, then outside in the crisp air, and then back inside. He tried to sit. He was too anxious for that. He thought about wiring the ranch but decided there was nothing to wire about just yet. So, he paced until he plumb wore himself out. It was about then he heard something that sent chills down his spine. Judy screamed. Loudly, and he started for the door, but thought perhaps that was not a good thing to do. When another scream reached his ears, he took two more steps toward the door, the nurse came out and rushed to the cabinet to get some towels.

"Is everything ok?" he asked her.

"Won't be long now", she said and rushed back to the room. In a brief time, the door was open, Brad got a glimpse of Judy's face twisted with pain and wet with sweat. What would he do if he lost her? So many women died in childbirth, of course, most of those didn't have a doctor standing over them, but still, it happened. Fear, anxiety, and panic began to grip his heart and he knelt and began to pray.

After about 10 minutes of silent prayer, Brad realized the office was quiet. He dared not move. What was wrong? Judy was quiet, he had heard no baby crying and no sounds were coming from the other room. *My God what was happening?* he thought.

Brad waited for another 10 minutes before the door opened. The nurse poked her head out and said. "You can come in." Her face was weary, and her expression didn't tell of anything wrong. As he approached the doorway, his heart stopped.

There in the bed sat his wife holding a softly cooing baby in her arms. Her hair was wet with sweat and had been smoothed down no doubt by the nurse. Her face had been washed and she beamed like Brad had never seen her. She took her gaze from that of the infant to her husband and softly said "Mr. Thompkins, come meet your daughter."

A GIRL! He had a daughter. She was so tiny, so very tiny that he was afraid to touch her for fear of breaking her. Brad stepped closer in awe of this little pink bundle. He touched the little fingers, and she grabbed hold of his finger. *So incredibly tiny!* he thought. Why, those little fingers didn't even go all the way around his index finger.

He shot a glance at the doctor with a questioning look.

"She appears to be a fine healthy girl, ten toes, ten fingers, one nose.... beautiful." the doctor said.

Brad beamed. She was perfect. Both his little ladies were perfect!

Before long, the nurse said, "Well now, these two need to eat and get some rest, so you men can go and us ladies will take it from here."

The doctor motioned for Brad to come with him, and Brad found it difficult to tear himself away, but finally kissed his wife on the forehead and touched his baby girl and walked out of the room.

"Doc, how about I buy you breakfast?"

"Don't mind if I do." the doctor said.

Over their breakfast, the doctor told Brad it would be at least three or four days till Judy was strong enough to travel, and then she should be lying down on the buckboard for the trip. Brad said that was not a problem. The doctor asked if he would like to use the other bed in that room while she recovered. He thanked him but knew if there was another illness or birth in town the use of that bed would be needed, so Brad politely declined.

The doctor inquired if they had come up with a name yet because if so, he would record it on her birth certificate. Funny, but the two of them had discussed a few names, but they really hadn't decided on one. For now, on paperwork at least she was 'baby girl Thompkins.'

He sent a wire home. It contained eight letters it read "IT'S A GIRL."

Chapter 25

The days passed by quickly for Brad and Judy after the birth of their baby. It took them over a week to decide on a name for their little darling girl. They finally settled on Fern Thompkins, in memory of those loved ones that she would never know. Brad had suggested it and Judy wasn't sure but when Brad looked at the baby and said, "What do you think Fern?" that baby smiled, or appeared to as it may have been just a gassy baby, for the first time. That did it. Fern Thompkins it was.

Fern was about 6 months old when they discovered there was indeed something not "quite right" with their little girl. They discovered that when she slept, nothing could wake her except a touch. They at first figured she was such a good sound sleeper, but when she was sitting on a blanket playing in the living room and a large vase was knocked on the floor just behind her; Judy noticed she didn't even flinch. They went back to the doctor to confirm but she was indeed deaf.

The doctor explained to them that many new advances had been happening with those who were deaf and if this beautiful baby had to have a malady, this was perhaps the best one to have. They got a book on a new invention for the deaf. They called it sign language, and it used hand motions to represent letters and words. Both Judy and Brad were determined to learn and teach their little girl this new language so that she might be able to communicate with the world when she grew up.

Fern grew fast and learned faster than Judy and Brad could. Before long she was talking a blue streak with her hands. Judy and Brad would have to slow her down so that they could understand most of the time.

As she grew, she grew lovelier every day. She had dirty blond hair that went just beyond her shoulders by the time she was 8. She was a delicate girl. She was nothing like her mother except in looks. She wanted to be rugged and strong, but she was frailer than her mother, and had a heart bigger than her father's. She couldn't hurt a fly and treated even the weeds in the garden with respect. Perhaps because of her deafness or perhaps because of the Godly teaching of her parents she had a nature that was quiet, soft, and made her all the more beautiful. People in town all protected the child as she grew. She was like the entire town's child by the time she was 16. Every boy in the area wanted to court her and for the first time in his life, Brad finally understood why Mr. Fern didn't want anyone to court his only daughter until she was much older. At all the church socials, she sat among a flock of young men. They even learned sign language just so that they might talk to her. She was loved by all.

Judy and Brad had not been blessed with more children. Perhaps God thought that one deaf child was enough. Perhaps, Judy, having only one child, was her price to pay for the sins of the past, even though she knew in her heart this was not the case. She often relived that horrible night in her mind. Either way, they were devoted to their little Fern. She was hardly little now and was such a blessing to them.

Judy had lost Mary the goat many years ago, about the time Fern was 3. Mary had lived a long life and given her three beautiful doelings. She died with a bout of pneumonia after giving birth one spring. Judy took it pretty hard. Mary had been her most trusted confidant. The two of them had been together since she was just a child. Judy gave up her dream of her goat herd after Mary's death. It just wasn't the same in the barn without her beloved Mary there. She sold all her goats for the price of a blackberry pie to a young girl, who, like herself, when she was that age, dreamed of a goat herd all her own.

Judy had made the deal with her fair and square, but she had to make the pie all by herself, with no help from her mother. When the pie was delivered, she was brimming with pride. Judy didn't have the heart to tell her the truth about the pie she had made. Apparently, the aspiring cook had forgotten to put in sugar, as the pie was a bit too sour to eat. She raved about it none the less at church the next day, and even poked Brat in the stomach when he said it was better than any pie he ever had! He sure earned that name! She checked in on the goats for a while but when she saw the young lady was doing right by them, she lost interest.

Judy focused all her time on Fern. She was being taught all the social graces that a child of moderate means should know. Brad had plans for her to go to a university, but Judy knew they would never take her. Her disability meant her life would be limited, but her father still dreamed big for her. Judy knew Fern longed to find a man like her father to marry one day. Judy also knew Fern was in no hurry. She had told Judy once; she wasn't about to settle for second best. She would wait for Mr. Right to come along. Some day he would.

Judy knew this to be true. When you least expect it, God gives you what you need most, even, as she had learned if you don't really want it. She was now about thirty-six years old. Brad was coming up fast on forty. By local standards, they were already starting on old age. Most men seemed to die in their forties or fifties. It is perhaps because the men worked so hard here in this part of the country. Some men made it into their sixties or seventies and some occasionally made it further than that, but most, it seemed, died fairly young. Many middle-aged women had been widowed young living here. She was pleased to see that her man was still a strapping hunk of a man. He was aging well. The gray at his temples made him look more handsome and one might even say wise. The gray in her hair that surrounded her face, just a few silver strands mind you, made Judy look old when she looked into the mirror, she thought. Especially, when she compared herself to her lovely daughter.

The air was thick with the smell of lilac on this beautiful late spring day. Judy asked Fern if she would like to go for a long walk with her to visit the grave sites by the old homestead. Judy didn't go here often because, even after all these years, the memory of that horrible day stayed with her. Fern loved nature and readily agreed to go with her mother. She let Brad, who was working at home that day on some needed barn repairs, know that they were going to the cemetery and the homestead and would be back in time for supper at the latest. Brad, busy with his current project, nodded his head in acknowledgment and went back to his work. Judy paused a minute thinking she should give him a peck on the cheek but thought better of it as he was working so hard, and his attention was obviously on some great calculation.

Judy and Fern walked together down the road, both admiring the beauty that only a spring day can bring. To watch all the world come back to life and to see the color bursting forth with such brilliance, always warmed Judy's heart. She loved this time of year; in fact, she could perhaps say it was her favorite.

She also had a great fascination as she watched the way Fern approached things. Without the sense of hearing, she noticed things that others did not. She would often comment to Judy how soft a leaf was, or how brilliant colors were, sometimes it was hard for Judy. How does one explain the sound a bird makes to one who will never hear it? Fern would never in her life hear the sound of the babbling brook, or of her children playing. How does one express the nature of such things to one who can never experience them?

Fern would try to understand when her mother reacted to the cry of a hawk as it flew over. She knew there was a sound associated with some things, but also knew that she could never fully understand them.

They stopped momentarily at the grave of Judy's father. Fern had been told all about her grandfather and the story of the awkward courtship between her father and mother. She would laugh when her mother would tell about the trapped/shot rabbits, and again when she told the story of the night she was born and the baby stuffed bunny her father bought for her. She still had that bunny tucked away in her remembrance box. She had only gotten a bit of information about her grandfather, but perhaps that was because he had died at a young age. She ran her hand over the course stone on the top of her grandfather's stone. He was a great man by all accounts from the stories of her mother and father. Fern watched as her mother talked to the stone. She could read lips and was even learning to communicate with the hearing community that didn't know sign language but knew this was a private moment between her mother and her grandfather. She walked to the edge of the fence and waited for her mother to be ready to continue on.

When her mother had finished, she touched Fern on the arm as she watched some of the local boys playing a ball game in a nearby field. Fern knew all the boys in town, and on another day, she might have gone and sat to watch the game, but today, she was spending time with her mother. She loved to be with her parents. They were kind loving people who, although she often didn't totally agree with their old-fashioned views, loved her more than their own lives. She knew that with her heart. Her father would yank on a hand full of hair to tease her when she was studying for a test. He always knew how to make everyone smile.

As they approached the old homestead, she could see her mother's countenance change a bit. She had been told many many years ago by her father that something very bad had happened here to her mother but was never really sure just what it was. It was something that no one would talk about much except to say that it still bothered her mother to this day and that is why they rarely went there. Apparently, it had been sold some years ago, but the folks lost everything in a hailstorm one year and moved away. Her father had bought the land back from the bank and had proper headstones put on her grandmother's and uncle's gravesites years ago. He even made a little white picket fence to go around the graves. It was a lovely place, the little graveyard. Once they had made their way past the old falling down farmhouse and barns, her mother's mood and posture changed back to the confident stride she usually had.

Fern left her mother to visit the graves and went just a short distance along the overgrown field to find some wildflowers. She loved picking them. They smelled wonderful and were so colorful. She would pick two large bouquets. One for the little graveyard and one for her grandfather's stone they would pass again on the way home. That would please her mother and Fern knew if she pleased her mother her father would also be pleased with her. She liked to please them.

Judy had told her father about her daughter's charm with all the boys. She also told him not to worry, that Brad was a good man who was watching those boys closely and besides Fern was a levelheaded girl. She now began to tell her mother how gentle and kind Fern was. She tried to express what joy the child brought to her and Brad, and how proud she would be of her granddaughter. She talked of the hard work she had put into learning at school, and despite her disability, she would graduate with her class. She talked about what a beautiful girl she was, and how she wished that she had gotten a chance to meet her grandmother. "She is a lot like you," Judy said to her mother's stone, "kind, gentle, yet hard-working and perseverant."

Judy had no words for her little brother. He had not lived long enough to be a friend to Judy, but she wished she had the chance to get to know him. As Judy dusted off her knees of the dirt from kneeling on the ground, she turned to see where that girl had gotten too. Judy could see her way off in the field, carefully going from one wildflower to the next making bunches of beautiful colors in her arms. "That's my girl" Judy thought.

She turned to leave the graveyard, and it was then she saw it. A great huge bear came lumbering out of the woods. It had no doubt been using the abandoned house or barn for a home, and as far as it was concerned, THEY were the trespassers. Judy looked back to Fern who was blissfully unaware of the grunting bear as it approached her mother. Judy had no way to signal her. Had no way to make her run as fast as she could for help. Judy exited the graveyard and stood by the little white gate built by her husband so many years ago.

The bear was huge. It must have stood 13 hands high when it rose up on his back feet and growled a terrifying growl, his yellow teeth glinting in the sun as though to show them off. The thick black fur waved back and forth as it began to trot toward Judy. There was nowhere to run, nowhere to hide, she knew she was the only thing between that bear and her daughter. Judy stood her ground.

This, she thought for a moment just before the bear leaped toward her, this was her atonement for her crime. She was paying her debt to God. She had taken a life and now she would protect one. She spread her arms wide and grabbed the bear with every ounce of strength she had. God was calling her home. Today was the day.

Her last thought as she hit the ground was for her daughter and husband. *I love you*, she thought, and in that very last split second, before she hit the ground in the arms of the enormous bear, she was finally at peace with what she had done so many years ago. God put it upon her heart to finally forgive herself for killing that bad man. Thank you, Lord.

Fern had just about enough flowers when she figured her mother would be ready to go. She turned toward the graveyard and didn't see her mother. She began to meander toward the little fenced in yard, picking more flowers along the way, when she saw something black. She wasn't really sure what it was at first. She stared at it for a while with her head cocked to one side trying to decide just what she was looking at. It was then that the bear picked up his head. She had never seen a bear up close, and this was a big one. He was sniffing the air and his nose was red a very bright red. *Dear God,* she thought almost screaming in her head. She saw the bloody scraps of her mother's dress under the bear. She tossed the flowers down and ran behind the old farmhouse. She kept looking back to see if the bear followed her. She ran all the way to town checking behind her all the way. She was not aware of it but had been screaming a muted sort of cry when she saw the boys still playing their game. She was crying, panting, and was shaking so badly that she couldn't sign to them what was wrong. One of the older boys ran to the ranch to get help.

When Fern saw her father, she ran to him. She had tears streaming down her face, and dirt and dust stuck to the trails previous tears had made. Her father was yelling something, but she was crying so hard she didn't understand what. He passed her to the pastor, who had joined the couple for supper; a growing crowd of ranch hands had assembled as well as some town men who had heard from their boys that something was very wrong at the old Fern homestead.

Her father and several men with guns and farm implements in hand were running down the road toward the old homestead several miles away. She knew what they would find when they got there. She knew her mother was in the Lord's presence now.

Chapter 26

Together they stood hand in hand and side by side. The tears were gone now. Well, not gone, but kept for only the private times when one can have too much time to dwell on things of that nature. Everyone had gone but the two of them. It seemed hard to leave. Brad looked down at the small hand in his and gave his daughter a sad smile. It was the best he could muster. How was he supposed to go on? He was not equipped to be father and mother to this child. Judy had been the one who had always known how to handle things where his daughter had been concerned. He stood looking at the freshly turned earth and the beautiful pink hue of the stone. Judith Fern Thompkins, it read devoted wife and mother of Fern.

She was really gone. How could she be gone? Other men had killed the bear that had attacked and killed her. She had sacrificed herself; Brad was sure, to save her daughter. That was how Judy was. As soon as the bear left to run at the approaching men, Brad had run to Judy. It was too late; it had taken them too long to get there and the bear had done way to much damage. The sight of her lying there was something Brad could never get out of his head. Every time he closed his eyes, he saw her that way. He prayed for the image to be stricken from his mind, but still, the image was burned into his memory. What was the last thing he had said to her? A grunt, a nod, he couldn't remember. Whatever it had been he was ashamed that it was not enough.

After he had returned with her mother's body, Fern had not left his side. She seemed scared and confused and Brad was not as good at making the signs as Judy had been. He didn't have the words to comfort her. Together they prayed, but he didn't really know if she knew how to pray properly. Had Judy taught her? How could he not know that?? Judy had always done those types of things; he simply had never thought of it before. Judy was such a good mother…. such a good wife.

Fern stood there beside her father at the graveside of her mother for a long time. Finally, she signed to him it was time to go. Her father nodded his head, and touched the headstone as though he was patting a soft kitten, then turned and walked home with his daughter.

That night neither of them ate, even though the house was full of every manner of food imaginable. People from miles away came to show their respects for Mrs. Judy Thompkins. Everyone loved her. They all brought some type of food to share, and after everyone had talked, offered condolences, and left, there was perhaps a week's worth of food left for the family and most of the ranch hands. Brad couldn't even bear to look at it.

The ranch house, once his comfortable home, now seemed like a tomb. Still and empty without her presence. The only light that shone was Fern as she went through the house trying to fill her mother's shoes. She was such a beauty. Such a good girl. What would he do with her? He knew nothing about raising a young lady. He was a rancher at heart. Judy had known that. She had learned to be mistress of the manor. She, with grace and beauty, had become the face of this place and his family. She was the one who worked tirelessly for the poor and helpless. She had been the one who always knew what Fern would need to be successful in life. All Brad had ever had for her were dreams, Judy had held reality in her hands.

Brad walked to the barn, but even that reminded him of her. There were no places where her spirit didn't linger, on this ranch. He wanted to get on his horse and ride, ride hard. He wanted to leave this place and never come back, but he knew he had more than himself to consider. He knew he had to live for Fern. She was Judy's gift from God. God had seen fit to leave the rest of the job of raising this fine young lady to him. He would NOT take that responsibility lightly. He would go on; he would fight to recover from this. He had to. He knew with God's help; he would go on to make his wife so proud of their little girl.

    Brad knew before he took his last breath on this earth, he would make sure his little girl was taken care of. Safe and sound, but he had to do something first. There was something he should have done long long ago. Perhaps if he had done it way back then this would never have happened, but he hadn't and now he regretted that decision. He mounted his horse and rode toward the homestead.

    When he arrived, the sounds of the night were all around him. The bear that had taken the life of his beloved Judy lay near the door to the old barn where the townsmen had killed it. The spot where she had laid still looked dark in the moonlight from her blood spilled on the ground. He stood there for heaven only knows how long, and then began his work.

    He grabbed the bear and tried to drag it into the barn. He soon found that he couldn't budge it. The massive creature must have weighed seven or eight hundred pounds if it was an ounce. He got a rope around its back feet and tied the other end to his saddle horn. Slowly the horse dragged the bear into the barn.

    Brad closed all the doors, broke up the paddock fence outside, which was old and brittle from so many seasons in the sun and weather. He tossed them at the base of the barn and lit a match. He set the barn ablaze. He then turned to the house and lit it on fire as well. He sat by the road with his horse tied to a tree and watched as the flames consumed the old Fern Homestead. He saw in the flames the faces of those who had lived, died, and been a part of this place. He watched the flames lick the sky and, in some way, felt as though he had released trapped and tortured souls on their journey to God, but deep down he knew it was his soul that was tortured and somehow, taking some revenge if even on a building, made things just a little better. The flames calmed him and brought him back on speaking terms with God somehow.

He saw his wife there as she had been many, many years ago, gathering hay for the winter for her silly best friend Mary the goat. She was happy, working hard there on the farm, she had been happy. Brad knew she had been happy with him too. And for the first time since it happened, he smiled as the vision of Judy came into view holding their child for the first time. Alone with the smoke and flames, he was content with his thoughts and dreams.

Tomorrow…he would begin his work…. the work God was asking of him. His daughter…. Judy's daughter…. was his priority now. From now on, Fern Thompkins would be his focus above all else. *You will be proud of me Judy*, he thought, you *will be proud of what our daughter will accomplish one day. As God is my witness, you will be proud!*

TEACHER

Chapter 27

When Fern awoke in the morning her head was fuzzy from the events of the last few days. She donned her mourning dress which was a modest black dress with black lace around the collar, cuffs, and hem. She hated wearing it, but it was what one did when a loved one passed away. She went downstairs and found her father sitting at the table. He still wore his hat and coat and smelled badly of smoke and ash. He motioned for her to sit at the table with him. She sat and looked at him. He was tired, worn out from losing her mother. She was his world and Fern knew it was up to her to give her father a new focus. To give him reason to go on with the life her mother so wanted him to have.

She let him take his time signing his letters. He spoke the words which was good because he was not as good at signing as her mother had been. He asked her in words and sign, "What do you want to do with your life Fern?"

The question took Fern back a bit. Her father had rarely asked her about her desires or wants. He had always left those discussions to her mother and then her parents must have discussed them later on she figured. Now with her mother gone, he needed to know from the horse's mouth, so to speak.

She took her time and signed slowly for her father. Twice having to find other words to explain as he didn't understand the proper sign for the word, but finally was able to convey that, her mother and she had recently talked about the thought of her getting a teaching certificate and opening a small school for young children who were deaf like her. She went on to explain she longed for a place where they might come for a month or two at a time to learn signing, and skills that they would need in school in order to learn and grow. In addition to that, she had heard some exciting news about new teaching for the deaf that was taking place on the East coast. Something about a new form of signing that was easier to learn and use. As it was, different regions used slightly different signs for things, and this caused confusion if a deaf person traveled. She had also heard about a deaf woman who was touring and writing, she wasn't sure, but she thought the women's name was Keller.

When she finished her father looked at her with a sort of funny grin. He told her that she was her mother's daughter. He had thought she would say settle down with a local boy and get married, have children, and live a quiet life, but, like her mother, she had grand thoughts and ideas and desires, and he was pleased with what she had told him.

He got up, removed his hat and coat, and walked behind her. Bent down and kissed her on the head, and then sat in the chair beside her. He looked at her and signed, "Where would you like to begin?"

Fern hugged her father and signed to him, "Daddy, today, let's begin by going fishing in that spot at the lake that mother loved so much. I will pack a lunch for us, and we can catch some of those nice mountain lake trout for our supper."

Brad loved this little girl so much. She was hardly a little girl anymore, he thought. She was a woman. But for today, on their fishing trip, she was still his little girl. He didn't bother to sign just said the words "Get out of that black dress and into some proper fishing clothes young lady!" with a smile.

She bounced up and ran upstairs. It was good, he thought, to see that bounce in her manner. "God," he said aloud, "tell my Judy for me that I will look after Fern and someday perhaps sooner than I know, I will meet her in heaven, and we will be together again. Oh, and Lord, make sure she knows I love her." A tear escaped from his eye as he got up and he wiped it away. There was no time for tears, he thought. There were fish to catch! He had to change too. All of a sudden, he could smell the smoky odor on his clothes from the fire. Life was going to continue….it always does, somehow.

The next day, Brad got up very early and went into town. He was there waiting for the wire office to open. When it did, he sent a cable to Dr. Leavy asking about this new form of signing on the east coast and what he could tell them about it, he also explained that his Fern wanted to open a school and wanted to be a teacher of the deaf. He sent a wire off to the state educational board as well. He inquired about when the next teaching exam would be given and how his daughter might get added to the list of students taking the exam. The last wire he sent was to the bookstore in Casper asking about a woman who was deaf lady that wrote a book by the name of Keller, or some such thing. His little girl would get what his little girl wanted and needed. Brad would make sure of it.

Before long Dr. Leavy returned a wire saying that, **Thomas Hopkins Gallaudet** developed American Sign Language (ASL). Inspired by a desire to help his neighbor's deaf daughter, Gallaudet went to Europe to meet with Laurent Clerc, a deaf instructor of sign language who was developing a more standardized form of signing for the deaf. He would write to him to inquire and to get any materials for Fern that he could. He added in the wire that he was pleased she wanted to do this and once established, he would be proud to recommend her school to any deaf patients he had.

It took a few days to get an answer from the other wires he sent, but Brad soon learned that an exam to become a state certified teacher was next offered on June 25th and it was a two-day, two-part exam, consisting of English Literature, Mathematics, History, Geography, Science and Chemistry.

The wire arrived on May 28th. That meant Fern only had a few precious weeks to study if she wanted to try this year, and since Brad knew nothing of most of those things, she would be on her own for this project. Judy would have known what to do, he thought.

When Fern heard the news, she was almost giddy. She rushed off saying something about her teacher, but Brad missed most of it as she went so fast! Before long she was bouncing down the road with several big books in hand. Apparently, the local schoolteacher had some of the books she had used to study for her teaching exam and allowed Fern to borrow them. "That's my girl," Brad thought, "just like her mother, self-reliant, full of energy, and so smart!"

The days passed by all too quickly for Fern. She had practically locked herself in her room for three weeks just to study for this exam. She was very good at Mathematics, and Science, but History always gave her a headache, and Chemistry was not routinely taught in rural schools such as the one she attended.

Dr. Leavy had offered a room at his home to Fern while she took her exam. Brad took him up on the offer, as this was the busiest time of year for him, and he would be sending her by coach. Dr. Leavy agreed to get her off the coach and escort her to and from the testing or if he was unavailable, he would make sure she was not left unattended in the big city. Brad knew this man well after all these years. Why, he had even attended Judy's funeral. He came all the way from Casper on the coach, just to offer his condolences. Tom and Brad had become good friends over the years, and Brad knew Tom was as happy to see Fern succeed as much he was. Why this man had been there the day she was born, was there to watch her grow, and had helped her bury her mother. Tom was a good man and Brad trusted him.

As promised, when the day came to take the coach to Casper, Dr. Tom, as Fern called him, was waiting for her at the station when she arrived. He greeted her with a big hug. He was almost like an uncle to her, aside from the fact that he was also her doctor of course. He had learned to sign very well and was full of questions for her. They silently talked all the way to his home. Most of the people looked at them as though they had two heads. They had never before seen this type of communication. He asked about how her father was doing, and about her upcoming exam, and he asked about all her plans for the future.

Dr. Tom had never married. His life as a doctor, Fern suspected, kept him too busy to have time to court someone. He was a good man, and Fern truly loved him, almost as much as her father. He had a modest home, but very comfortable, and Fern was excited to be in the city again.

The teaching exam was scheduled for 7 a.m. tomorrow. Dr. Tom told her he would walk her to the testing site, which was at the university located at the other end of town, and then be back when they had their lunch break to take her out for lunch. She couldn't wait to see the university for the first time. She asked if he would be able to stay just long enough for her to get checked in in case, she had any trouble. She could speak a little, but it was not always understandable to those who were used to hearing speech normally, and rarely used it. He agreed of course and told her that in case an emergency had come up and he was unable to meet her he had planned for his friend, a local shop keeper to meet her instead. He had thought of everything.

Tomorrow was a big day. She retired early and found that sleep was hard to grasp. Her life had been going in a whirlwind since that last day with her mother. She knew things were going to change for her, and she was excited for what God had in store for her. She found herself walking down the road again with her mother in her dreams. This time, however, they talked about the future, about her father and Dr. Tom, about heaven. She was happy there in heaven her mother said but missed us…. We miss you too mom. It was then that the dream ended, and she awoke to a new day and perhaps a new future.

Chapter 28

The day had finally arrived. She dressed and went out to find Dr. Tom making scrambled eggs and coffee for breakfast.

"If there is one thing us doctors get plenty of in lieu of payment, it is EGGS!!" he said.

They ate and then headed out for the university campus. When they arrived, Fern was shocked at the size of the buildings. They were massive brick structures with several floors. There were at least three separate buildings, and Dr. Tom said they had plans for a fourth building to be built next year. Students bustled about like ants going here and there all talking and carrying loads of heavy books. Fern already felt like she simply didn't belong there. Seeming to sense her apprehension, Dr. Tom put an arm around her shoulders and gave her a little hug. The line for the teaching exam was very long. Now she felt bad for asking the doctor to wait till she got registered before he left her. She told him she would likely be ok, and perhaps he should go, but he said no he was proud to wait with her. After all, he told her, she was the best-looking lady here, and why wouldn't he want to be seen with her. She blushed and scoffed at his teasing.

The other people waiting in line looked at the two of them strangely. Most, she thought, had never before seen someone who talked with their hands. She smiled graciously at those who made eye contact with her. They smiled back but were confused as to what they were doing. Fern could read it on their faces.

The line moved rather quickly and within about 15 minutes they were at the registration desk. Fern filled out the entrance card and passed it to the clerk.

"Your date of birth?" the clerk said without looking up.

The doctor answered for Fern as she didn't see what the clerk had said as he wasn't looking at Fern when he said it. The clerk looked at Fern as she asked the doctor in sign language what had been asked.

"Sir, what is wrong with your daughter? Is she deaf and mute?" the clerk asked.

"He is not my father." Fern said. She talked slowly so she would sound out her words correctly. "He is a family friend. And to answer your rather rude question, sir, I am deaf, I am, however, NOT mute."

"I am sorry Miss…," he looked at the paperwork, "Thompkins, but this exam is not set up for people with your…well your…. infirmity. I am afraid you will not be able to take the exam."

The doctor began to speak, but Fern silenced him. "Good Sir," she began, again talking slowly to sound out her words well, "In an effort to get this rather long line moving, would you please show me where it states in writing that deaf persons are excluded from taking this exam. If you can do that, I would be happy to leave, however, if you are unable to do so, please allow me to register and take the exam."

He shook his head and gave her a number. "We will see," he said. "I wish you luck madam, you're going to need it."

They stepped by the registrar's table and the doctor looked at her with immense pride in his expression. "My God," he signed to her, "You are JUST like your mother. "And he laughed.

She asked if her words sounded correct and he assured her that not only did they sound correct, but her indignant tone came through rather well.

"Your parents would have been proud of you just now. And your physician is also proud of you! Now young scholar, you go in and show them what you're made of. I will meet you by the statue we passed out front on your lunch break." With that the doctor turned and left her.

She walked into the auditorium and found a seat near the front. This way she thought she could read the lips of those giving instruction for the exams. It was about quarter till and people were still coming in. Just before 7 a.m. they closed the doors and Fern figured that everyone that was taking the exam had arrived. She counted about 45 students in all.

At precisely 7 a.m., an older gentleman walked up on stage and began arranging papers behind the podium. "Thank you all for coming today to take the state certification test to become a teacher within our state. You must understand that most of you will not pass these exams. They are not designed to be easy. We want only the best caliber of teachers, and to that end, we have designed this exam to be the hardest test you have EVER taken. If you do not pass this time you are allowed to retake the exam next year when it is offered again. The proctors will begin now to pass out the first part of the exam. It is in Mathematics. Do not open your test until you are told to do so. Failure to follow ANY of the instructions given to you will result in immediate removal and failure of the exam, and cheating will result in immediate removal and failure of the exam. The proctors are all professors here at the university. If you have a question about a test question, raise your hands and one will attend to you promptly. They will be walking about the room throughout all the testing to assure no one is cheating in any way. Each test is given 2 hours to complete, if you finish early, you can close your test booklet and sit quietly until the time has elapsed. Bathroom breaks will be given between exams. Once you begin an exam you will not be allowed to leave the room until the test section is complete. Leaving the room during an exam period will result in immediate removal and failure of the exam. There will be two tests given this morning in Mathematics and Science. There will be a lunch scheduled from 1 a.m. to 1 p.m. At exactly 1 p.m. the doors will shut for the afternoon session. Failure to be back in this room when the doors shut will result in immediate failure of the exam. This afternoon's session will be a two-hour exam in Chemistry and a two-hour exam in English. At 4 p.m. you, you will be dismissed for the evening. Tomorrow you are expected to be here in your seat by exactly 7 a.m. Failure to be here tomorrow at 7 a.m. will result in immediate failure of the exam. Are there any questions before we begin?"

Fern looked at the test packet that had been placed in front of her. It appeared to be constructed of many pages. This she thought was only the mathematics section. She straightened her posture in her chair, said a silent prayer, in which she told God she wanted to make Him and her mother and father proud, and she waited for the signal to open the packet and begin.

The signal was given when the man on the stage said "You may begin. You have 2 hours."

Chapter 29

The examination was tough, tougher than Fern had figured it would be. She struggled with some of the questions and even second-guessed those problems that she knew and did easily. The second part of the morning session was the science section. Fern found most of this easy, but toward the end of the test, she began to run into sections that she hadn't studied or had never heard of. She did her best to come up with decent answers all the same. No answer is definitely a fail, at least if she put something down, she had a chance to get credit for it.

She kept watching out of the corner of her eye at the stage. She did not want to be still working when they called "time" for fear of being expelled from further testing. She had expected there might be an issue for a deaf person to take this exam. She had practiced what she would say if such an issue arose. She was pleased with herself when the clerk did not turn her away.

When the science section had finished, Fran still had several questions unanswered. She worried about how the grading worked and was concerned that she might have already messed up her chances of becoming a teacher one day. Dr. Tom did his best to reassure her, but still, she felt as though somehow, she was less smart than the other students who were taking the exam. They all had an air of confidence about them, as though they already knew all the answers and were just taking this exam as a formality of sorts. Fern had no such confidence. She fretted over each question and panicked when she found a question, she was unfamiliar with.

When the afternoon session resumed, at least one person did not return. The girl who sat next to Fern in the morning session had not made it back in time or had simply given up after the first part of the test revealed how difficult this exam was to be.

The chemistry exam led off the afternoon session. This was the test Fern dreaded most. She had spent long hours going over the textbook her schoolteacher had let her borrow. Surprisingly enough, she found that this exam was perhaps easier than the two she had taken this morning. When she finished before time was called, she looked about the room to see every other student busily working. Fern began to worry that perhaps her answers were too simple, perhaps she had not grasped what needed to be put down. She began to go back over the exam to check her work when the man came back to the stage and called time. She hoped she had done well. At this point, it was all she could do.

The English exam was lots of spelling and grammar and the usual types of things one would find on that type of test. By the time that test had ended, Fern was all but worn out. Her head hurt from thinking, and her hand was a bit cramped with all the writing. Her pencils were worn down to nubs and needed proper sharpening.

After Dr. Tom and she had supper, she went right to bed. She fell asleep almost at once. She woke up and dressed hurriedly. When today was over, this would all be behind her. She found a note on the table that said, 'Fern got called away in the night for an emergency. Someone will be here at 6:30 to bring you to the school. Good Luck! See you at lunchtime. Dr. Tom'

Fern searched the house for a timepiece. Dr. Tom had used his pocket watch yesterday to know when to leave. Suddenly Fern thought, what if she slept too late, what if the person had come and gone when she didn't answer the door. In a panic, she searched the small house and finally found a mantle clock in the parlor over the fireplace. The time read 6:25. She placed a hand on the clock and felt the tick-tock of the movement inside and knew that it was a working clock and not one that had been left unwound for days on end. She went out on the front porch to sit and wait for her escorts to arrive.

Finally, after what seemed like hours a friendly-looking lady came and smiled at Fern.... she looked directly at her and very slowly spoke the words. 'I am here to take you to the university.'

Fern had all she could do not to laugh and wondered if she was speaking loud so that this poor deaf child might understand her. People were funny. Fern had run into this many times, but usually after several meetings, people stopped treating her as different. It didn't bother her because she knew that they did it out of kindness and no understanding of what deaf people were like. This lady didn't know how to communicate with sign and only wanted Fern to be at ease and understand her intentions.

Fern walked fast and the poor woman had trouble keeping up. She was NOT going to be late for class today. The lady had a lovely little timepiece on a broach that read 6:50 when they arrived at the university. Fern turned and thanked the lady for her troubles and hurriedly went inside to go to her seat.

When she arrived, she found that most of the people were already at their desks and several people were milling about on the stage. Two of the men kept looking toward Fern and then talking more. She was unable to tell what they were saying as they were partially turned back to her, but she figured it likely had to do with the fact that they didn't expect her to show back up today.

At precisely 7 am, the doors were closed, and a man approached the podium that had not been there yesterday. It was clear to Fern he was a man of some importance as he carried himself differently than the others, and the others seemed to defer to him. He began to speak.

"Good morning, I apologize but there will be a slight delay in testing this morning. You will be given the full 2 hours each for your History and Geography exams this morning, and after the lunch session, our professors will grade your last two exams. Those exams you took yesterday have already been graded. At approximately 3:30 pm, you will be assembled here, and we will announce those students who have passed the examinations and will receive their teaching certificates. That being said, he turned to look directly at Fern, "Miss Fern Thompkins, may I speak with you outside for a moment."

Ferns' heart pounded in her chest. What had she done wrong? Had she done so badly on yesterday's exams that they wouldn't allow her to continue? Had someone thought she cheated? She was suddenly terrified. She rose slowly, looking around the room and all eyes were on her. She followed the man outside feeling like she was walking to the gallows.

When he got to the door to the hallway, he motioned for her to go through first then shut the door behind him. He then turned and faced Fran.

"Miss Thompkins, I assume you read lips well as you have made it this far but am I correct that you are deaf?" the man said.

"Yes," Fern said aloud, "that is quite correct, Mr........"

"Pardon me," he seemed a tad flustered to hear her speak and Fern wondered if her speech was poorly spoken. He continued, "I am Sectary Bruce Rinds from the Education Board for the state of Wyoming. I am here because there is a concern that you wish to gain a teaching certificate. After all Miss Thompkins, how could you possibly conduct a proper classroom? Without hearing, you wouldn't know when students were cheating, you wouldn't hear questions when asked, and it simply doesn't seem feasible for you to become a teacher. Surely you must have thought about this. "

Instantly Fern was angry. She took a deep breath, regained composure, and began to speak as eloquently as she possibly could. "Mr. Rinds, it might interest you to know, that my aspiration to teach does not include a "regular classroom of students" as you put it. I am endeavoring to develop and begin a learning center for those, like me, who were born deaf or lost it due to an illness or the like. My goal, dear sir, is to try to erase the typical response, such as you are exhibiting here today, that because of the lack of hearing I or we are somehow less capable or less worthy of a normal life. Furthermore, unless my grades from yesterday's exams were sub-standard somehow, I would appreciate the opportunity to continue."

Mr. Rinds looked at her for a moment. "Tell me Miss Thompkins, is your father Peter Thompkins by any chance?"

Fern looked a bit puzzled but answered the question. "No sir. My father is Brad Thompkins; my grandfather's name was Peter."

"Ah yes, that makes sense, you would be a granddaughter, wouldn't you. Tell me, how is Peter?"

"I regret to inform you; my grandfather passed away a couple of years before I was born. Might I enquire as to how you might know of him?" Fern was really puzzled. After all, her grandfather, by all accounts she had ever heard, was a fairly big name in their little town, but hardly a well-known figure.

"Oh, I am sorry to hear that." Mr. Rinds said, "I don't know what you have been told about your grandfather Miss, but your grandfather and I helped to make this state a state. Why, if he hadn't been so devoted to that little spread of his in that backwater town, he would likely have been one of our state's first senators. He was a good man, and I am deeply sorry to hear of his passing. I can see a bit of his fortitude and self-confidence filtered down to his granddaughter as well. All right Miss Thompkins," he straightened and put his official demeanor back on, "I will allow you to complete the exam; however, you must know that you will be given no special considerations, nor will your grades be judged any differently as those of all the other students."

"I would expect no less, kind sir." Fern said and for a moment it almost seemed like in her mind her mother had said those words.

"Then shall we go back and begin?" he said, opening the door and motioning for her to return.

The other students looked shocked to see Fern reenter the room and she knew they were all wondering what had happened out in the hallway. She took her seat and soon the final day of testing began.

Chapter 30

During the lunch break, Fern was already tired. Dr. Tom met her as promised and over lunch, at the diner, she told him all about the meeting with Mr. Rinds. Dr. Tom offered to go and speak with them about the situation, but Fern said she thought it was taken care of, so she was just going to wait and see how she did on the testing. She told the doctor what they had said about not needing to go back till 3:30 that afternoon for the results. Dr. Tom said if she would allow him to, he would like to go with her to the results as he knew they allowed the family to wait outside the auditorium. She told him she would love to have him there…after all, to her, he was family. She thought she saw the slightest glimpse of a tear begin to well up in the old doctor's eyes, and then he said that he was done with his lunch and if she could find her way to the house, he would meet her there about 3 this afternoon.

Fern took her time and finished her lunch. When she went to pay for the meal with the money her father had given her for the trip, she discovered the doctor had already paid for her meal. She walked through the busy streets and saw the bookstore that her father had wired a few weeks ago. She decided to see if the book she had inquired about was available. She had a bit of difficulty with the clerk there who insisted upon talking with his back turned to her, but eventually got the information that Miss Keller was writing a book, but it had yet to be released, and they would notify her when that became available. Well, she thought as she left the store, so much for the reliability of the local town information chain. Well, at least she knew the true story now.

She successfully found her way to the house and made herself a hot cup of tea and tried to let her anxiousness fade into the cup. What an amazing development to meet someone here that actually knew her grandfather. She wished she had met this man. He sounded like he was really a remarkable man and she wondered why her father had never spoken of his efforts to gain statehood before. Dr. Tom seemed surprised by the news as well, so she surmised he knew nothing of it either.

When three pm rolled around and Fern saw the doctor coming up the street, she was already raring to go. How had she done? Was it good enough? Would they honor the conversation she had with Mr. Rinds and award her the certificate if she passed. Would they fail her and not tell her that it was because of her deafness and not because of grades. Those and so many other questions loomed about in her head. The doctor could see her tension and signed to her that it would be fine, no matter the outcome. If she didn't pass this time, she could come back next year and try again.

When she got into the room you could have cut the tension with a knife. Every student sat upright and silent waiting for news of the outcome of this grueling ordeal. The parents and guardians who were in attendance were asked to remain in the hall as Dr. Tom had said they would do. She stared at the door that the moderator had been using to come and go throughout the last two days. Before long, the moderator came to the podium and began to speak.

The following names are those who have successfully passed the teacher's certification tests. Please know that your certificates will be sent to you in 1-2 months in the usual post. Those who do not hear your names will know you did not pass and can return next year to retake the exam should you so choose. I will say that we have an exceptional bunch of future teachers sitting here in the room today. I congratulate you all on your aspirations to teach. Now, to the business at hand: Abigale Abrahams, Toby Acers,"

OH GREAT, Fern thought, they are going alphabetical. I will be waiting till near the end.

"Sarah Dunn, Polly Ebeser,"

Only up to the E's this was going to take forever. Fern bit her lip till it hurt to keep from bursting at the seams with anticipation. Each time a name was called everyone, but Fern heard a little cheer or excitement. Fern saw the faces though and knew those whose names were being called.

"Gordon Slocome, Diana Sly, Bertha Tabalot,"

This was it; they were down to the T's…. Fern watched closely as each name was called. Why was THOMPKINS so far down the alphabet!

"Foster Tony, Glenda Vigner, .and last but not least Jeff Zimmson.

They didn't call her name. She had failed. Fern's heart sunk in her chest; her stomach had become suddenly queasy. All that work, all that studying, and all for nothing. She had failed. Her dream seemed so far removed from her now. She raised her head to see that the moderator was still speaking, she really didn't want to know what he was saying, but she tried her best to take this defeat with dignity.

"So after having said that, we have one more person who would like to address all of you new teachers. Mr. Rinds, secretary of the Education Board for the state of Wyoming."

Mr. Rinds took the stage and shot a quick glance Fern's way. He was no doubt pleased that she had not passed. They didn't want a deaf teacher in the state, to begin with.

"First, I want to congratulate all those whose names were called we are glad to have you all as new teachers to the young people of our state. Now I wish to impart to you all that you are a witness to history today. Today, for the first time in this state's history and perhaps the country's history, a deaf person had successfully completed the examinations to become a certified teacher in the state of Wyoming. Miss Fern Thompkins will you please join me on stage."

Fern's mouth dropped open, she stared at Mr. Rinds on the stage, and she couldn't move. Somehow, she managed to rise and start up the stairs to the podium. When she turned around every person in the room was applauding and one by one they all stood to their feet and continued to clap. She had passed. She was a teacher.

When the volley of applause died down and everyone was seated, Mr. Rinds continued to speak. "Miss Thompkins has plans to provide those in this state with maladies such as her-self with proper education. We at the education board would like to thank her for her dedication to the deaf citizens of this state. Her certification will of course be restricted to the teaching of the deaf, but we are all proud of your accomplishments here today. "

The applause began again, and Fern almost missed the part about "restricted to the teaching of the deaf," which she was not happy with. If she passed then she passed, why should her deafness make that accomplishment any less, but she knew it was a big gain for not only her but the deaf of the state.

When she told Dr. Tom, he smiled from ear to ear. "I knew you could do it." he signed. On the way back to his home, they stopped and sent a wire home. It said MISS FERN THOMPKINS, TEACHER, and nothing more. *Daddy will be so proud,* she thought.

That night when she laid down her head, she said to herself. I am a teacher. I am really a teacher. Thank you, Lord. Eventually, the excitement of the day faded, and sleep overtook her.

Chapter 31

When Fern arrived home, there was a fanfare awaiting her at the coach depot. Everyone in town turned out to welcome home the state's newest teacher. Fern couldn't help but shed a few tears at the overwhelming kindness and love shown by everyone in the town. They even had the church choir singing, Hallelujah! Her father met her with a big smile and signed the words, 'I knew you would do it! I love you so!' After all the congratulations were given and her father and she were walking to the buckboard, he said he had to show her something, and they would not be going right home.

Fern was a bit curious, but after the overwhelming outpouring from the town, she couldn't imagine what he might have to show her that would compare to such a welcome as she had just received.

They rode through the town as well-wishers waved to them. Fern couldn't help but smile. She was so happy and felt more blessed than she had ever been. As they rode out of town, she was thinking of the last few days, the emotions had been such a wide range of fear, anger, anxiety, and joy. She was so overwhelmed by it all. She tried to get her father to tell her where they were going but he just smiled and said, "you will see."

All at once, she realized they were headed in the direction of the old homestead. She had not been back there since it had happened. Why would he take her there? She was a bit apprehensive about what she might see. Did he not know that the sight of the place would bring back horrible memories?

As they approached, Fern looked at her father with confusion. The old cabin and barn were gone. Judging from the surrounding field they had burned. She was even more confused to see several bunks of lumber sitting on the site and some of the ranch hands digging in what appeared to be a cellar.

Her father stopped the buckboard and handed her a piece of paper. "It's about time that something good happened on this land. It has seen its share of tragedy, now it will be used for something truly wonderful, and in God's plan I am sure of it."

She shook her head to show she didn't understand, and her father pointed to the paper he had handed her. She opened it and began to read. It appeared to be a deed to 60 acres of land and the title was in the name of …. It was at this point that she began to cry she could hardly read the words on the paper: Thompkins Institute for the Deaf.

"It's yours, Fern." Her father said "I will build you a school. It's all yours."

Fern, still crying, and beginning to cry harder, said aloud as best she could given her tears "Thank you, Daddy, I love you so much" with that her father began to cry as well.

"Wait till I show you the plans Fern." her father said, "It will be a two-story structure with a basement. There will be rooms for students to stay, rooms for teachers to stay, classrooms, a dining room, a big kitchen, even one of those water closets. We will put this land to good use. God has a use for you darling. Your mother and I always knew that. You are special in my eyes and in God's, never forget that."

She looked toward the tiny cemetery, and it no longer had a wooden fence, but now had a lovely wrought iron fence surrounding the gravestones. They had buried her mother next to her mother and brother. Fern knew now why they had done that, the action confused her at the time, but now it made sense. Her mother would be here to see her school. She would see her daughter grow and her ambitions spring forth.

Fern knew this was the beginning of something big. It wasn't going to be easy. She knew that, but she would triumph. She knew that as well. She would start her school; she would teach deaf children to live in a hearing world. Someday deaf children will be looked at just like any child, not as their disability. Someday, Fern thought, Someday, she would help make it happen.

Chapter 32

Joshua Whittier walked with his seven-year-old son to the stream. He held his hand. He didn't know any better than to run off, he was only seven and was totally unaware of the dangers of the world. Joshua sat beside the stream and watched his little boy play. How had he made it this far with this little boy? When his mother had died on the day he was born, Joshua had cursed God for taking her. He refused to talk to God ever since then. He knew that his life was missing that comfort that God used to give him, but how could he ever trust in a God that would take his lovely young wife and leave him with an infant deaf son to raise?

Tomorrow he would take Seth to a strange place and leave him there. How could he do this? After all, Joshua was all the family this little guy had, but how could he not try to do all he could do for him. He was the boy's father and he loved him. He didn't know how to help him. He tried, oh my how he tried, but he couldn't see the world how his little boy did. Joshua could hear birds, hear the rushing water of the stream, hear the splashing little Seth was doing, hear him laugh; Seth couldn't hear any of that. He didn't understand when he was doing something unsafe because Joshua couldn't explain to him why he can't touch fire, why you can't go in the same pen with the bull, why a little boy shouldn't touch a gun. Joshua feared for his son's wellbeing if he did nothing. It wasn't fair to him. So, when he heard about a new school opening specifically for deaf children, he got in touch with them right away. Tomorrow he would take Seth to this place. He knew his little boy wouldn't understand why he was leaving him. He knew someday he would, but not now. So today he spent the day with him. Playing and having fun.

Joshua hoped he would remember this day spent at the farm and not the vision of his father walking away and leaving him with strangers. Joshua would visit as often as he could, of course, but how would Seth understand? Joshua really didn't understand, except that he couldn't handle him. He threw temper tantrums because he was frustrated not knowing what his father wanted from him. Joshua knew why but didn't know what to do or how to communicate with him. He knew he was a good boy. Joshua knew in there somewhere there was a good boy. The little angry child who he lived with now was and could not be his son. He knew that somewhere in the mind and body of that boy was his son…his real son who could be a good boy.

He felt like a heel. He couldn't even explain to Seth where he was going or that he would be back. UGHHH…. I am a bad father. Joshua knew that with all certainty, he was the worst father in the world. There had to be someone out there that would help his son. He knew he couldn't. He wanted to, but he couldn't.

God was to blame for all this. God took his wife. God had given him a deaf son. God had it out for him, he thought, and he struggled with figuring out what he had done to deserve all this sorrow. People told him, "God has a plan for you." He scoffed at that notion. God evidently was out to ruin his life, and he would never forgive Him for that.

The time was getting late. Joshua motioned to Seth that they needed to go. Seth began to yell and showed he didn't want to go. Joshua took the boy by the hand and started to lead him down the path toward the house. The boy pulled away and ran back to the creek. He tripped at the edge and fell into the shallow stream. Seth was angry and falling in the water made him even more upset. Joshua ended up carrying the boy kicking and screaming and soaking wet to the cabin. There has to be a better way. There has to be.

Chapter 33

His little girl had been taught to sign, but she still struggled. She had lost her hearing after having scarlet fever. It was that disease that took her mother, and for the first 5 years of her life, she was able to hear. Then all of a sudden that part of the world had been taken away from her. Suzie was a beauty like her mother, dark brown hair and at 12 she was just coming into her feminine features. She had learned to sign, yes, but she resisted any attempt to teach her what the hearing world taught. She would become angry and say that a deaf girl had no hope of anything so why should she even have to learn? She felt that no one would want to marry her, no one would want to employ her, and as far as she was concerned, her life was over at the tender age of twelve.

Lawrence Cooley wanted her to grow, wanted her to learn. Why, did he even showed her in the newspaper where a lady who was deaf got her teaching certificate, but she said that was a fluke and that was one out of thousands. What does one token lady mean? She would say. Lawrence, or Larry as most called him, knew that to a certain point she was right. What would a deaf girl do in life? Who would want to marry her? He had written to the teacher named in the paper and to his surprise she wrote back saying she would soon be opening a special school specifically for the deaf. Perhaps he thought that would be different for his Suzie. Perhaps if she got to meet people who were also deaf and were doing something with their lives it would be different. He prayed every night that he would hear soon from the lady opening the school as she promised to wire him with a date when she would be ready to open. When that wire came, Larry was so happy. Suzie was not impressed at the prospect.

Suzie had accused him of trying to get rid of his "special" daughter. She accused him of trying to hide her away so that he might be able to find a new wife and be happy again without her in his life. Larry had tried to tell her that was not the case. He tried to explain that he thought it would be a good thing for her to learn and he would come and see her often and she would have friends and fun, but she was hearing nothing of it.

Larry eventually got mad at her insolence and told her she WAS going, and she WAS going to deal with it until he believed it no longer needed. He was her father, and he knew what was best for her. She ran into her room in tears, and Larry knew no way to console her. Tomorrow they would go out on horseback for the four-day trip to the new school. *She would thank him one day,* he thought. Perhaps she would even find a boy she liked and who liked her. Maybe if she liked it, she would want to become a teacher like this lady, Thompkins, was her name. Maybe she could even be employed by this school. There was a lot to contemplate. Suzie hated him, but she would see. This was all for the best. He prayed he was doing the right thing.

Suzie cried and cried. Her father was ashamed of her. She knew this to be true. Suzie knew that no lady would want to marry her father when she was around. She knew that he had been alone for too long and wanted to meet someone nice, but who would want to marry someone with a child like her? She tried to keep to herself; she tried to help out here at home. She couldn't understand why her father thought it important for her to go to school. Why should she, what did she need to know that she couldn't learn here. She was destined to be nothing but a burden to her father for the rest of his life and after her father was gone, she knew she would be that scary spinster witch that the little children made fun of. Why had God done this to her, and her father? Why does He do bad things to kids? Suzie didn't understand. She knew her father would make her go to this school for deaf kids like her, but she didn't have to like it. Maybe if he got rid of her, however, he could live a normal life again. She loved her father, but it still hurt to think she had to be put away for him to be happy. She continued to cry till sleep finally overcame her sorrow.

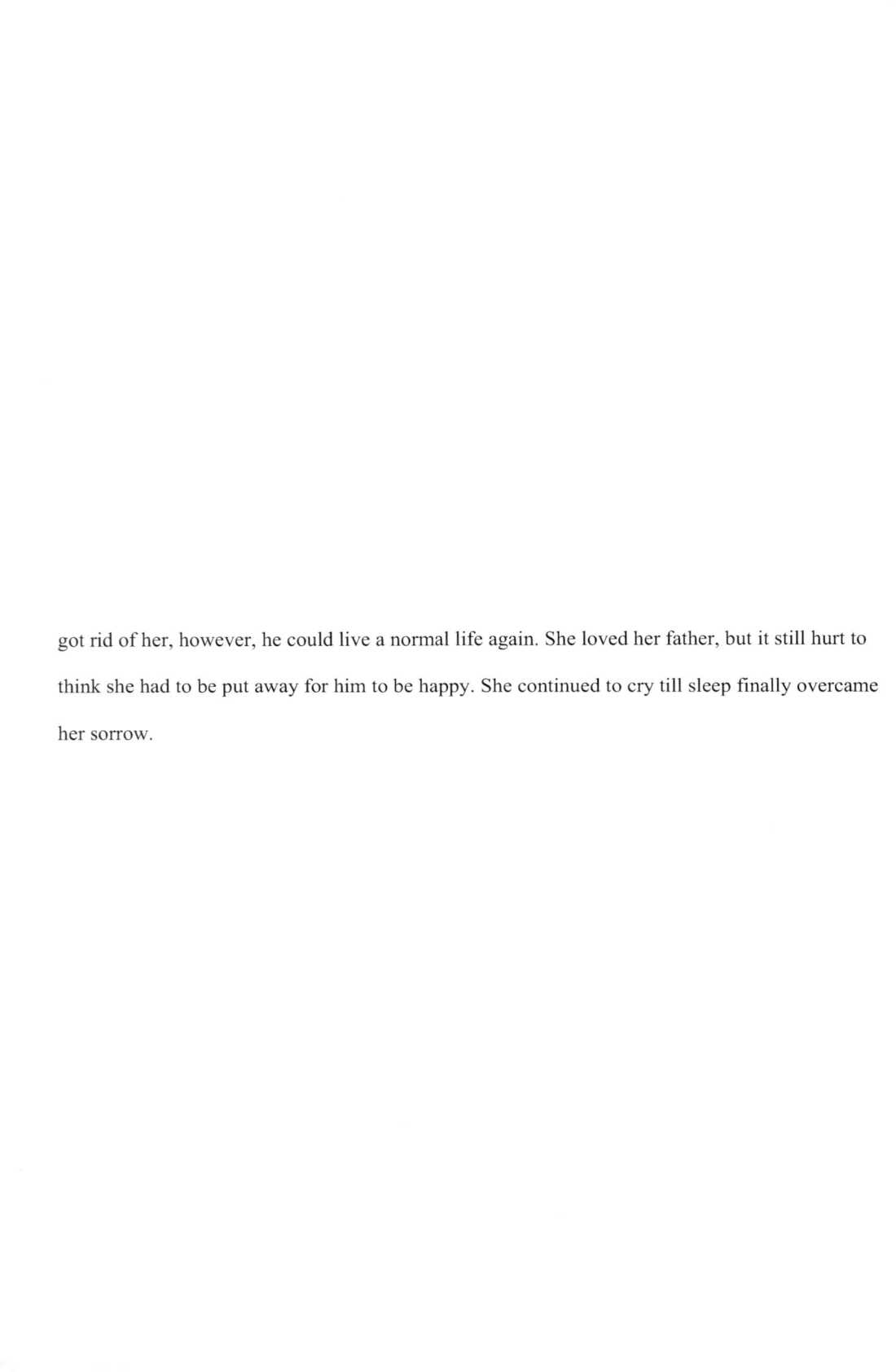

Chapter 34

Fern watched with wide-eyed wonder as the school began to take shape. She had already been contacted by 4 students and so that would be her first class. They had all seen the article that was originally published in the Casper newspaper about her gaining her teaching certificate. She suspected her dear doctor friend had perhaps prompted the original article. It was then picked up by several smaller papers throughout the state and from those her students came. They all wrote their stories of woe. She had led a rather privileged life and didn't really realize how much so until some of the letters came explaining the dangers and worries of these parents. *God protect my students*, she thought, *till they can get here and be safe*. One, maybe two had learned a little sign language and she couldn't wait to get their assistance to help the other two who had never been introduced to it. She was so excited that next week her school would be open.

The last coats of paint were being put on; the icebox had been brought in, the stoves installed, the beds, tables, and desks were made and put into place. It was really happening. She would soon be a teacher with students all her own. She knew it would be difficult, but she knew God would help her and her new charges to excel in whatever He had in mind for them. She had written to the newspapers of several major cities in the state and had told them about her new school in the hopes they would provide some free advertising for her. Only one did, and that was a few lines in the around the state column. She did let other deaf institutes in the country know that if they got any contacts from people in her state that she was a certified teacher and would be taking on new students.

Four students were a small start, but it was a start. Perhaps if she did wonderful things with these others would come. Two boys and two girls were coming on Tuesday of next week. The boys were seven years old, and twelve years and the girls were eleven and twelve. She knew she would have her hands full in the beginning, but she could handle it. She prayed she could anyway. Her father offered to "help," but she told him he had done so much already and enough was enough…she was on her own now. She knew, however, if she got into trouble somehow, he would always be there.

She had officially moved out of her parent's home and into the school. This was to be her new home. Her father had provided her with a set of dishes that he paid way too much for. They were a beautiful service for twelve made of the finest china that had a lovely blue flower pattern on them. She wanted to put them away for "good" and get some tin dishes for the school, but her father said, "These people will be paying you good money to board their children here. They should have a few luxuries like fine china to eat off."

Perhaps he was right but several of the letters she had received said the children were angry and some threw temper tantrums, she wasn't sure how she should deal with behavior like that, but decided God would tell her what to do when the moment happened. She was excited, scared, and happy all at the same time. She would spend the weekend wandering about the house and grounds and looking for things that needed tending to or sprucing up.

Her time had come, she knew that. She went to the tiny graveyard and told her mother about her new students. She knew her mother wasn't there, really, she was in heaven with God, but she had seen her mother do this to her grandmother's grave so supposed if it was good enough for her mother there must have been something to it. She longed for her mother. She wished she could have been here sharing her joy and helping her to learn to deal with children, especially deaf children. Her mother had been so patient with her. She hoped a little bit of her patience had rubbed off.

She walked by the place where her mother had fallen when she was attacked by the bear. Her father had planted a bed of flowers on that spot. Her father was such a good man. He had turned a horrible spot into a lovely place. She smiled when she looked at the beautiful flowers and the little plaque which said, "Judy's Garden." Her mother would have loved this. She had a small area on the side of the new building for a garden, and although it was a bit late, she figured she and the children could get a little fresh food from it before the season was over. She smiled when she saw the little pea pods beginning to form and the cucumber plants just starting to trail. They would have some nice fresh cukes before long and that would be a welcome addition to the menu. She would, with the children's help, prepare all the meals. The store was agreeable to bring out the needed groceries twice a month, and she knew the town was not too far off should she need something special. Everyone, well almost everyone, in town knew a little sign language because of her growing up here. That would surely make her charges feel welcome should they need to go into town. Everything was in place. The time had come. Tuesday was coming fast, and her school would be open. She was a teacher, and now she had to prove it.

Chapter 35

Fern and her father waited at the school. Her father had asked one of his hands to take any of the students out by buckboard that arrived on the coach today. Judy had been told that at least one was riding on horseback to the school. The excitement was overwhelming. The stage had arrived and three of her students were supposed to arrive on it. She watched anxiously for the buckboard to come up the road.

Her father pointed to the road when he spotted the buckboard in the distance. Fern rose from her chair and got ready to greet her first students. Brad was so happy for her. He looked at her and saw so much of her mother in her. He had gone into a bit of debt to make her dream come true. He had to sell some of the family holdings to make ends meet, but in the end, it would be worth it. He was keeping his promise to God and Judy. He had totally focused on his daughter. She was not letting him down. He had spent so much time working here that his cattle herd was suffering, and he knew that soon he would have to go try to salvage what he could. Nothing mattered to him but her happiness. He had made a mistake once by leaving his beautiful wife when she needed him most, and he had neglected to be there for her when the end came. He would not make those kinds of mistakes with Fern.

As the wagon approached, Fern could see only two little faces peeking out and three parents. She wondered if the other student had missed the coach. She greeted her parents with sign language greetings and her father interrupted her with words. This was easier for the parents and the children could see what signing looked like. She began:

"Welcome to the Thompkins Institute for the Deaf. My name is Miss Fern Thompkins, and this is my father, Mr. Brad Thompkins. We are so happy to have you here to be the first students at our school. We hope to accomplish many things here, but first and foremost we hope to teach your children to talk, via sign language such as I am using now, and to learn to read lips so they may communicate well with the hearing world and would learn all the things that would be taught in a traditional school. We are also going to explore avenues of employment for our students when it comes time for them to leave. This is not designed to be a permanent placement but a stop along the way for your deaf children to adapt to a hearing world. They call us deaf and mute. That is a poor choice of words. We are not mute. We are as intelligent as the hearing; we just need to process information differently. Here your children will learn to do that. Now unless you have any questions for me, I have a lovely lunch prepared for you all."

The hired hand gave her a wire while her father fielded a question about when they could visit their children. The letter read: Miss Thompkins, I regret to inform you that our daughter Elizabeth will not be attending your school. She was killed in a fire at our farmhouse last week. God Bless you for what you are doing.

Fern began to tear up but decided that would not bode well for her new guests and told herself to plaster a smile on that face. Elizabeth had been the eleven-year-old that was to be company for Suzie who was arriving later that day on horseback with her father.

The two students who did arrive were Seth, a seven-year-old, who judging by his table manners had been given only slight instructions in right and wrong, and Peter the twelve-year-old boy who knew a small amount of sign language and longed to learn more. Peter was excited to be here. Seth was angry and it showed. His father was at his wit's end and that also showed on his face. Fern prayed that she might help them both become a family.

During the lunch conversation, Peter's parents were talking about how he had a basic knowledge of signing but some of his signs were not correct, they suspected. He had lost his hearing when his father was working in a mine only two years ago and Peter had wondered in to close to one of the blasts. He had been trapped under debris and had broken his leg in several places. He walked with a limp. Apparently, both his eardrums had burst when the blast went off. It was a miracle that he had survived at all Fern thought. He had a passion for learning before the accident that had left him deaf and that hadn't changed once he found he could continue to learn. Fern signed to him that they would be good friends, she was sure of it and that she hoped he might help her to teach the younger Seth from time to time. Peter eagerly agreed.

Seth's father, Joshua, told of the loss of his wife at the birth of his son. Fern could tell by his face as she read his lips that he had never gotten over that. She could also tell that he loved his son. He told about things he had tried to help his son but had no knowledge of what to do for him. He was most grateful for Miss Thompkins' school and for the chance to help his little boy even though he knew the boy didn't understand what was happening. Brad assured him that his boy would be just fine and that his daughter had the patience of Job when it came to children. Fern looked at her father and smiled. "That was my mother, and my father who have always given me much too much credit sometimes, but we will do right by your boy. Rest assured he is in good keeping."

Fern explained that it was not only the students who would get homework. Each parent would be given a booklet of the new American Sign Language hand gestures for them to learn so that when they came again, they could begin to talk to their children. Fern explained that these were the signs the children would be learning, and some other forms of sign language existed, but she was trying to assist the deaf community by teaching the standard signs they taught on the east coast and the premier deaf learning facility in the country. The three parents in attendance assured her they would study hard and learn to speak to their children properly for the first time.

By the time they had finished eating and had gotten the tour of the place, the last of her pupils arrived via horseback. Suzie and her father had been on the trail for four days and they looked it. She offered them something to eat but they respectfully declined saying they had stopped and eaten on the way here. Fern caught them up to speed with things and signed a welcome to Suzie. She reluctantly replied but was obviously not happy to be here. Her father sighed and walked to greet the other parents.

Fern let them know that since the stage only came once a day to their town there was accommodation in town if they wanted them, but she felt it best if they said their goodbyes today. She told the parents they could come every two weeks if they wished but asked that they wait on this first visit till a month had passed. This she figured would allow the students to get acclimated and settled down enough to really have begun to learn. The parents all looked worried, as Fern would have been, leaving her child with what amounted to strangers, but they all agreed to wait till a month had passed before they came. The three parents who came on the coach would get rooms in town; Suzie's father said he would just head back this afternoon and get half a day ahead of schedule.

When it came time for them to leave, Peter's mother was in tears, and Peter assured her he would be just fine. Fern thought this was a smart young man who she could really make strides with. Seth on the other hand was going to be a problem. He wanted to go with his father. He didn't understand when his father made a sign that evidently meant he had to stay. He began to yell and cry and tried to go with his father. Brad stepped in and picked up the boy and tried to comfort him. It was all he could do to hold the flailing boy. When his father finally rode out of sight, the boy stopped fighting and just let Brad hold him. Brad set him on the ground and took his hand and the boy was crying. The poor little fella didn't understand. He looked up at Brad and Brad smiled and patted his shoulders to try to convey it would all be ok. The boy wasn't so sure.

Suzie gave hugs to her father but was somewhat standoffish, and Fern wasn't sure what that was about just yet. Lawrence, her father, came to Fern and asked if he might speak to her for a minute. Fern agreed and they walked toward the flower garden and the tiny cemetery so that they might talk alone.

"Miss Thompkins," he began, "My daughter is quite sure I am trying to get rid of her. She believes that I am ashamed of her. Now nothing could be further from the truth, but she thinks I don't want her around because it is keeping me from finding another wife. I didn't know how to tell you all this mess in a letter so thought it best to wait till I could talk to you in person about it. I love my daughter ma'am, and I would gladly be a widow for the rest of my life if I could get her to understand that just because she is deaf doesn't mean her life is over. She thinks no one would ever want her as a wife. Now I don't begin to guess the minds of others and I don't know if that might or might not be true, but that is no reason for her not to learn."

Fern used her words in response and Lawrence was a bit surprised to hear her speak for the first time and quite well considering she had never heard someone speak. "Sir, I have been deaf since birth. I have always been asked to dance at the church socials, and so shall your little Suzie. All she needs is some education on what it means to be deaf and how to overcome the obstacles she must face. She will be fine. I will do my best to reassure her that you do love her, and I am sure when you return in a month you will see a big difference in her. May I ask you what you do for a living?"

"I am a cattleman ma'am.," he responded.

"I suspected as much. I have grown up amongst cattlemen my whole life and I just know one when I see one!" She laughed and he smirked a bit.

"Yes, I suppose we do have a certain "air" about us don't we." And he began to laugh as well.

With that, he took his leave and Suzie watched as he rode off trotting her empty horse behind him.

Fern gathered up the children and led them inside. She escorted the boys to one room and Suzie to another. Peter was asked to help Seth with unpacking and getting settled, and he promised he would. Fern helped Suzie and then told the two older children that they may wonder about the house exploring a bit if they kept an eye on Seth while she got their supper started. This is how it begins, Fern said. This is how it will begin.

Chapter 36

The first few days were a bit of a rough time for Fern. She wanted to begin from the basics of the alphabet with all three, but the older children already knew some of the signs and Seth didn't want to learn, but with the older children's encouragement before long he was signing his name. This was a big step for him. I think the day he finally did it right Suzie and Peter were as happy as she was.

Before too many days went by this ragtag bunch was beginning to be a family of sorts. Fern was so pleased. It wasn't too long before she had discovered each child's actual grade level and was developing individual lesson plans for them.

Seth was seven years old but was at a preschool level. Fern was sure he would catch on fast once he got the hand of letters and spelling and reading, but for now, he was way behind the others. He got frustrated and occasionally would do his whole temper tantrum thing. She had instructed the other students to ignore him when he did this, and she did her best to ignore him as well. Before long. he found that, unlike his father, this person didn't care about his fits, and he was left tired, sore, and still having to do the thing that started all the fuss, to begin with, and so gradually with time his fits of anger got less and less of a "show". He still would get angry and frustrated but as his understanding of what was being asked of him grew and his level of education grew, he found the more he learned the more able he was to understand, and he found the praise of his teacher and the other older students was much better than being angry.

Peter was Fern's little helper. This boy was smart. Smarter she suspected than herself if the truth be known. He was only twelve and he was working at a ninth-grade level. His deaf skills were lacking in places, but with each day that was growing better and better. He often finished his assignments early and would help the other students so that Fern could attend to some chores. This boy had potential for sure! She asked him one day what he hoped to do with his life. He said that once he had dreamed of being a doctor, but that now he knew that dream was gone. Fern looked at him and said…." hey young man, before me there were no deaf teachers. I am the first. Why couldn't you be the first deaf doctor?" She told him she would talk to her father about finding someone who might help him to learn to speak well with the hearing that didn't know sign language, just as her mother had done for her. She was sure she could find someone to help with that. And she would help him to get better at lip-reading too. He was thrilled to think that there still might be hope for him to become something wonderful in life.

Suzie had turned into her challenge, she was learning, there was no doubt about that, but didn't really feel as though it was anything more than a waste of time. She was also quite convinced that her father wouldn't come back when the month was up. She was trying to make the best of what she thought was a no-win situation for her, but she was sad in her heart and that was evident to Fern.

Each Sunday morning all four of them would walk into town and attend the local church service. She would sign the sermon for the children and before long even little Seth was asking questions after church about what the preacher has talked about. Their long walks back to the school usually consisted of rehashing the sermon and figuring out just what the main message the preacher was trying to convey. After church, each child had assigned tasks. They had them on weekday afternoons too, but these Sunday chores were usually less chore-like when they could be: Gathering items from the garden for Sunday supper, picking berries for pies, or even reading a story to Fern while she prepared the meal. Her father usually came to Sunday dinner and occasionally the new pastor and his wife came too. The elderly Pastor Tolle had passed away last spring and this new young Pastor Geddies was just what these children needed. Why, he had come asking to learn to sign so that he might be able to better support his flock. His wife, Emily, was charming too. She was such a refined lady. Her family had come from back East and evidently, they were not impressed that she had married a penniless preacher and moved out west. It was obvious to Fern, however, that she loved him greatly. Fern hoped that one day she would find a love like that. Like the love her father and mother had shared.

For now, her priority was these children and their education. As the day approached that the parents were due to be back, she worked with the children to supply a special presentation by each one of them to show how far each of them had come. Peter had planned to try out his new signing and talking skills in an oral presentation. It was strange talking without hearing himself and it took him a few days to find the right tone and volume. As it turned out, the hearing teacher who had taught Miss Thompkins offered to help Peter. She was a super nice person and worked with him twice a week on his diction and speech patterns. Seth would do a book report and Pastor would interpret for him. Since Pastor only read sign at about the level that Seth signed it was a good pairing. He had read a story in the McGuffey first grade reader, called 'The Little Know It All.' It was only a very short story and only the second one he had read, but he was so proud of his new skill and wanted to show his father. Suzie couldn't decide what to do, she didn't expect her father to come, so she said she would find something that the others might enjoy. She decided to sign how to make chocolate chip cookies since the recipe included some of the math skills she had been working on. Fern wasn't fond of that idea but decided that if it was important for her than it was ok.

The children worked practicing they projects every afternoon for a week until they could have presented them in their sleep, and Fern wondered if they were reciting them in their sleep because as she looked in on them at night they were quite often twisting and turning. Their excitement was high in anticipation of seeing their parents, and even Suzie began to dare to hope her father would come.

Chapter 37

The day had arrived. The students were far too excited to think about schoolwork today, so Fern busied them with chores and cleaning until the arrival time of the parents. Fern had written to all the parents in mid-month telling them how their children were doing and letting them know the date for the big reunion. Her father had not been around much during the daytime as he was working hard again on his business. Once he saw Fern had things well in hand, he had gone back to being a cattleman again. He was there today, as he said, he wouldn't miss the children's presentations for the world.

All the preparations had been made, and the children and Fern and her father sat patiently as possible, awaiting the buckboard to come up the road, much the same as Fern had done only a short month ago. Suzie wasn't sure if her father would come or not but figured he wouldn't be taking the stage as he didn't like to spend money on things like that. She decided to wait in the back where she could see the way they had arrived originally.

Seth was so excited when he saw the wagon coming up the road that he almost jumped off the porch rail rather than use the stairs. Once his feet touched the ground, he was off and running toward the wagon. Peter laughed and before long both Fern and her father were laughing too. When he got to the wagon his father jumped off and the two of them hugged and laughed. Fern could see his father sign slowly but sign the words "I love you, son" to Seth. Seth beamed as this was no doubt the first time the boy had ever heard this from his father. "I love you too Daddy," Seth said back and Fern could tell from a distance Joshua was crying. She was brought to tears herself.

Peter waited for the wagon to stop before beginning to sign fast, telling his parents all about what he had been doing. He was so excited that his parents had to tell him to slow down so they might be able to keep up. Peter's mother looked at Fern who had tears still in her eyes and signed "Thank you." Fern was overcome with emotion.

The Pastor and his wife had hitched along for the ride out to the school and had told the parents about the children's smiling faces in church every Sunday.

There was a man on the seat with her father's hired hand, who she didn't recognize at first. When she looked closer it was Lawrence, Suzie's father. Fern motioned for him to follow her and when they got to the edge of the house she pointed to where Suzie was hopefully watching the edge of the woods for her father to appear on horseback. Lawrence nodded a thank you to Fern and walked to Suzie. He was almost upon her when she realized someone was coming toward her. She turned and when she saw her father, she at once began to cry tears of joy. She was so sure he wouldn't come. She had hoped, but she figured he had moved on with his life. She hugged him so fast and so hard his hat flew right off his head. He bent down and whipped the tears from his daughter's face and told her with sign that "I promised I would come; I don't break promises sweetheart. Not to my best girl." With that, they both began to shed a few tears. Fern, looking on from the corner of the house, simply continued to cry, as she had right from the first sight of the parents.

When all the hellos were said and the group was back together, they all went to the shady glen where the picnic tables had been set up and began their picnic lunch, complete with fresh cucumbers from the garden, and a lovely pie made from berries the children had collected. When the meal had finished the children went off to prepare for their presentations. The parents were so pleased with their children's progress. Fran couldn't be more pleased.

Lawrence and Brad had wandered off a bit and were talking about something quite intently. Fern wasn't sure just what it was, as they were turned in such a way as to keep her from reading lips. Lip reading was a wonderful way to "spy" on people but today that skill wasn't paying off for her. Whatever it was, she could see her father put on that serious face he had when something very important was being discussed. She surmised that, since they were both cattlemen, they were likely discussing some cow-related illness or tips of the trade or some such related topic. Her father sure knew his cattle.

The children's presentation went well and the only student she had to correct their signing during the whole presentation was the Pastor. His wife Emily said she wouldn't let him forget that lack of concentration for a while! All of the children were beaming with pride at their presentations and Peters' parents broke into tears because it, they told Fern later, had been the first time they had really heard their son's voice since the accident had happened. They were thrilled. Suzie's father asked when her presentation was over if he might get to sample some of those cookies and she gladly passed around the plate of finished cookies she was using as a demonstration to those in attendance, with her father getting the first one.

Seth's father, Joshua, pulled Fran aside and told him that he was amazed that such a transformation had taken place in his child in such a short time. "Ma'am you have to be a remarkable woman." He said. Fern knew she was blushing when she thanked him. Similar comments came from Peter's parents as well. When the time came to leave, all the parents promised to come again when they could and would let Miss Thompkins know when they would arrive. When they were readying to leave on the wagon back to town that evening after supper, Joshua and Peter's parents boarded the wagon and Fern noticed that Suzie and her father were talking at the picnic tables. Her father came out and told the hand to go ahead and that he would take the other parents into town when he left in a few minutes. Fern looked a bit puzzled at this but suspected they wanted to talk shop more on the way back home. Men and their work she thought.

When Lawrence and her father finally were about to leave, Lawrence looked at her and said "Thank you, Miss Thompkins. It has been a delightful day."

"Oh," she replied, "please call me Fern."

"I would be right please to do that Fern, and I would like it if you would call me Larry, Lawrence seems so stuffy. Not like me at all" and he smiled.

Fern nodded in agreement and threw her father a kiss goodbye and watched as they walked away leading her father's horse. It was a fine night for the walk into town, she thought. Perhaps she might even take a walk herself later when the children were in bed. What a wonderful day it had been. All the parents were happy, the children were happy, and God had blessed her with so much love and praise today that she was totally exhausted from the day's events.

She looked at Suzie who had joined her and was standing by her side. Suzie put her hand in Fern's hand and looked at her with a smile. "See she signed to Suzie. I told you your father would come."

Suzie didn't reply but just beamed at Fern. She was such a lovely child when she smiled.

Fern had things picked up in short order and before long the children were fast asleep in their beds. Fern decided to walk no further than the porch and sat and enjoyed the night air for a bit before going to bed. She had peace in her heart she had never felt before. This is what God had intended for her. She was sure of it. She was meant to be on this porch, breathing the night air, in this spot at this moment. Her world was perfect.

From a distance, eyes watched Fern on the porch. She was lovely, there was no denying that. The eyes followed her into the house as she locked up for the night. Just her and the children all alone in that house. The eyes watched as Fern turned out every light in the house, and the silent night sounds and darkened shadows of each object within sight were all the eyes could see. Now was not the time……but soon…. soon yes…. soon.

Chapter 38

After breakfast the next day, where the previous day's events were rehashed, Fern announced that She was low on some dry goods and would need to go into town for a few things. The children begged to go with her, but she told them they needed to maintain their studies to impress their parents next time they saw them. She left them with some math problems to do and instructions should they finish early to read any book of the bible and be ready to explain to her what it was all about. She would often do that on Sundays too and the children loved comparing notes on what they thought of each piece of scripture. There were few books currently at the school, an issue Fern hoped to change soon, but for now, they had the good book and could use their spare time reading that.

The air was clean and fresh, as a late summer day can be in the early morning. Fran took her time walking along the road slowly as she knew the children would be fine while she was away. They had become so close, almost like sisters and brothers and they looked after each other when she couldn't be there. Peter liked being put in charge, maybe a bit too much, so today she let Suzie handle things while she was away. The trip into town found many of the town folks coming and congratulating her. Apparently, the Pastor and the parents had raved about her and her school all the time they had waited for the stage. It was so nice of the Pastor to see them off like that; she made a mental note to thank him if she saw him.

She bought her items and was about to leave town when she saw what she thought was a familiar face. Lawrence Cooley, Larry, she corrected herself, was riding into town from the direction of her father's ranch. How odd that he didn't leave on the stage with the other parents.

She waited for him to come near and waved at him to catch his eye. "Larry did you miss your stage?" she inquired.

"No ma'am. I should have told you last night but didn't want to make you think I would be interfering in you teaching my little girl, but your father has hired me. My other employer had sold off all his cattle and I was looking for work. Your daddy said he could always use a man with experience like mine and so I hired on with him. He was even kind enough to let me make up a bed in the tack room until something better came along." Larry said.

He sits on a horse proudly, Fern thought as he spoke. So that's what those men were discussing yesterday. "I guess you two were talking business. Always happens when you get two cattlemen together" Fern quipped.

"Sure does, Miss Fern, sure does. You needn't worry though. I will come at the normally scheduled intervals like all the other parents. "Larry said, "Your daddy is a good man Miss Fern," he added, "I am right proud to know him."

"He is a good man, Larry. Now if you're this close, you are welcome to come share Sunday supper with us. Suzie would love it. And as you may be aware my father joins us when he can." Fern said.

"I will surely try to do that; it would be a pleasure if your father doesn't keep me to busy that is."

"Well, if he does, I will just have to speak to him about that." She smiled and then said goodbye and continued on her way home.

She thought about this man most of the way home. He was not a particularly handsome man, but there was something about him and his way that had Fern thinking of him. What was it about him, she thought? He had looked very nice in the traveling clothes he had on when he came to see Suzie. He was good to his daughter and Fern knew he loved her very much. There was something about his eyes, she thought. Something lying behind those eyes she couldn't quite place. Black as coal they were, but not in a bad way. Something about his manner was different than other men she had been around, and growing up on the ranch she was always around lots of cattlemen. He was just ...well.... different. All the way home she tried to figure out what it was, but finally decided she needed more time to figure that mystery out.

Again, the eyes followed her. From the woods, they hid behind trees and bushes to watch her progress. She couldn't hear, so as long as they remained out of sight she would never know. The eyes watched as she scuffed the dirt along the road. She was thinking about something which was obvious. They watched as she decided to take the short cut her mother had told her about through the woods. The eyes saw her stop to pick some mushroom growing just inside the forest line.

Now was not yet the time. The eyes watched till she arrived at the school and brushed the dust off her skirt and shoes before entering the residence. The eyes stayed glued on the school for a long while. No, now is not the time. Not yet.

Chapter 39

The months flew by quickly now for Fern. The Sunday suppers with her father and Larry and the children were always a delightful end to the week. She and the children loved sitting by the wood stove in the parlor, while the men told tails of their cattleman days and all the excitement of the range. She watched her father when Larry was talking. She saw genuine respect in his eyes. She had become good friends with Larry, and it was obvious that her father thought a lot of him too.

Before she knew it was late November and she was saying goodbye to Peter and Seth so that they could join their families for Thanksgiving and Christmas. Fern had decided school was important, but family was important too and she wanted her small class of charges to be with family at that time of year, so she adjusted her teaching schedule to accommodate slightly more than a month off for the holidays. It was hard saying goodbye to the boys, but she was glad they would be back after the New Year began. It was decided that Suzie and Larry would join Fern and her father at the school for the holidays. After all, this was the town they lived in and Larry was still living at the ranch, Fern saw no reason why they all couldn't enjoy the holidays together. She loved that little girl and was amazed at how her learning attitude had really turned around this fall. She was eager to learn and even talked about getting her teaching certificate one day. Fern wasn't sure just what had caused the turnabout in her but was pleased to see it.

Thanksgiving saw Fern and Suzie working together in the kitchen to cook up the enormous turkey that Larry had shot while out checking fences on the ranch. The bird was far more than the four of them could eat, but Fern already had plans for some tasty leftover meals.

They all prayed a prayer of thanksgiving before their meal that day, everyone but Larry who said, "The good Lord knows my mind and what I am thankful for, as I tell him every day." Suzie's prayer sent tears to Fern's eyes and even to Larry's as she said "I thank God for Miss Thompkins and my father. I love them so and am so grateful He led me to this school."

Fern and her father went into the woods one Saturday after Thanksgiving to find a suitable Christmas tree. Larry had taken Suzie into town to do a bit of shopping and Fern enjoyed the chance to be outdoors with her father. She watched as he labored to chop the tree down, they had picked out. He was beginning to show signs of age, she thought. He was still a healthy man, but the gray in his hair and the deepening wrinkles on his brow told her that he was getting older. He was still the most handsome man she ever saw. A daughter's love for her father is a special kind of love that never ceases. He is the first man she will ever love, and she strives to find a man with qualities that remind her of him in the man she will eventually marry. Before she knew it, she had gone to him and hugged him.

"Whoa, what's that all about" he inquired.

"I just love you, daddy." She said and kissed his cheek.

"I love you too darling," he said with love in his eyes.

Once they got the tree back to the school, they fashioned a stand for it and placed it in the parlor. Brad had brought the box of ornaments he and Judy had made over the years they spent together. There was not a huge assortment, but what was there was special. Each ornament told a story or a part of their lives. Each one meant something, and decorating the tree became a wonderful trip down memory lane for Brad. When he got to the little heart with his and Judy's name on it, he remembered making it by the firelight of the old Fern homestead farm. The first winter they were snowbound here in that old cabin was a fond memory for him. He easily remembered her face when she first looked at the ornament he had fashioned. One would have thought it had been made of gold the way she fawned over it. *She was a special lady,* he thought as he hung it on the tree.

Fern saw that faraway look in his eyes and knew he was once more thinking of her mother. She knew better than to interrupt his memories, so she left to pop come corn to string.

By the time she came back with the corn and cranberries to begin string, he had finished putting the box of ornaments on the tree. He was grinning when he handed her a bundle tied up with string. "Here, this one I made for you. To begin your box of memories", he smiled.

She untied the string and found a little carved sign with a ribbon on top that said Thompkins Institute for the Deaf, below that he had put the year. She was amazed at how lovely this was. Why, it must have taken him months to carve out those letters so beautifully and so small. She proudly hung it in a place of prominence on the tree.

Later that evening after Larry and Suzie had returned, they all sat and strung popcorn and cranberries. When they had finished the tree was a thing of beauty to behold. Suzie asked about several of the ornaments and her father enjoyed telling her about each one and its special meaning. She thought it lovely how he treated this little girl as though she was family. To Fern she was, but it was obvious her father had grown to love this little girl.

That night as Fern sat and admired the tree in the parlor late into the night, the eyes watched. Closer this time, from just outside the window of the parlor the eyes looked upon her beauty. She sat and just looked at the tree as though it was speaking to her. It began to snow and for fear of leaving tracks the eyes reluctantly left the school, not yet, the time was coming, but not yet…. soon…. very soon.

Chapter 40

When Suzie awoke Christmas morning, she immediately went into Fern's room to see if she was awake. When she found Fern's bed empty, she bounded down the stairs to find her father and Fern and Mr. Thompkins all sitting at the table having breakfast. "About time baby girl," her father said with a smile. "We thought you would sleep clean through Christmas day!" They all laughed, and Suzie sat at the table trying to peek into the parlor to see the tree. She knew she was expected to have breakfast first, but eating was the last thing on her mind.

Before long she had finished her toast and egg and had a glass of cocoa. She anxiously awaited the signal to open presents and see the tree and stockings. Eventually, Fern said, "Who would like to go see if dear Santa Clause filled the stockings this year?" Suzie's hand shot up fast. The men laughed and they all rose from the table. Suzie was the first in the room. She waited for the ok to take her stocking from where it hung and when her father said it was ok, she eagerly began taking the contents of the stocking out and laying it on the table. She had an orange, a rare treat out this way, two peppermint sticks, a fifty-cent piece, and a new jump rope. She was giddy as she could be. She was already thinking of what she might buy herself at the store with her money as she began to peel the orange.

The adults watched her as they all smiled. There were a few presents under the tree, and before long they had all been opened. Her father and Larry had both gotten a new sweater that Fern had knitted for them. She was so much better at knitting than her mother had been at her age, Brad thought with a chuckle remembering the scarf with the holes and uneven ends she had fashioned for him that first Christmas. He still had it at home in a drawer.

Suzie got several games and a scarf and hat, and mitten set Fern had made for her to match her winter coat. She immediately put them on while she ate her orange. Fern received a package labeled to her from Suzie. She acted shocked when she saw Suzie waiting for her to open it. "I picked it out for you myself," she signed to Fern. It was a lovely broach. It had a silver butterfly sitting on a tiny silver branch. It was the loveliest thing, and Fern rushed to the girl to hug her and thank her for her thoughtful and beautiful gift. On her way back to the chair, she nodded to Larry her appreciation as she knew he had bought it for the girl to give to her.

Before long, the tree was bare of gifts, or so Fern thought.

Larry pointed, "There is one more present I think Miss Fern, just over there toward the back."

Fern looked and sure enough, there was one more small bundle in the back. She practically had to crawl under the tree to retrieve it and when she had done so and turned around both Larry and her father were laughing at her. She was blushing to think of how that must have looked from their perspective!

She waved at them as if to say, 'stop that,' and looked at the tag on the gift. 'To Miss Fern from Larry'

She looked at Larry with a puzzled look and sat down in the rocker to open the gift. When she opened the bundle, inside the cloth was a small box. She again looked at Larry with a puzzled look. She opened the box and found a ring, a ring with a diamond on the top.

Her mouth dropped open, and she looked from Larry to her father to Suzie and back to Larry again. He rose and went to her, got down on one knee, and said "Miss Fern Thompkins, months ago I asked your father for your hand. I knew the moment we spoke that first day I took Suzie to this school that you were the woman I wanted to marry. Your father told me I could stay here and work for him so that I might court you, but I found it hard to tell you how I was feeling and would quite often look upon you from a distance as you walked home from town or sat on your porch at night. I wanted to be close to you, wanted to tell you how I felt, but I am not good at those types of things. So, I decided that if you might consent to be my wife eventually, we could have any length engagement you might find suitable. I am a patient man Miss Fern; I love you and I know Suzie loves you. When I talked to her about having you for a new mother, she was so excited I thought for sure she would give my secret away. She did well not to slip all these months. The more I got to know you through Sunday suppers and long conversations, I knew without a doubt you were the only woman on God's green earth that would make a suitable wife and mother for me and my girl. Now I don't expect an answer right away. Take your time as I am sure you never really considered me in that light, but if you would at least take this token and give it some thought I would be most grateful. I guess that's all I have to say. Will you consider it Miss Fern?"

Larry had spoken his words and Fern had all she could do to keep her attention on reading his lips. She gazed at his eyes and looked at the man kneeling on the floor before her feet. She saw a man who, it was obvious to her, loved her as he said he did. She had grown to look forward to his company. She enjoyed the time spent with him; she was sure she loved Suzie as a daughter. She already considered her family. Tears began to well up in her eyes as she shifted her gaze from Larry to her father. He nodded his head as if to say "he is a good man" with one gesture. She looked at Suzie who, as soon as her gaze met hers, slowly walked to her father's side and knelt beside her father and added, "Won't you please be my maw?" She signed.

That was more than Fern could take, she began to weep. Larry stood his ground. He stayed kneeling and placed a hand gently on her hand that held the ring. Fern took the ring out of the box and looked at it. It sparkled in the light that streamed through the windows on this cold Christmas morning. It was beautiful. She put the ring into Larry's hand and extended her left hand so that he might place it on her finger. "I would be most honored to be your wife and Suzie's mother, most honored." With that, Larry placed the ring on her finger and stood. He pulled her out of the chair and offered her a hug. Suzie was not to be left out and hugged them both.

Brad looking on from the settee, thought how like her mother she was. How Judy would have liked this man. He was about to gain a son, and one day he would leave his business to him to run. She would continue to have her school, and now Brad knew his job was complete. He had made a promise to Judy and God to see to it she was taken care of. Larry would take over from here. He had a good head on his shoulders; he knew the cattle business and loved his daughter as much as Brad loved Fern. They would make a good life together.

Brad knew looking at the three of them that no matter when God called him home, he would be ready. Fern and Larry had many challenges ahead of them, Brad knew that. Something told him that like his Judy and himself, there would be tragedy ahead, sorry, heartbreak. No one escapes that in life, but like himself and his beloved Judy, they would have each other and that is all that anyone can ask for. That one person in the world who knows you better than you know yourself, who loves you more than anything and would gladly lay down their lives for you, as his wife had for his daughter. Fern would have that now.

Judy, he thought, he often spoke to his wife in his thoughts, *do you remember that kind of love that you can see in his eyes? I remember looking at you with that loving look at each and every time I looked at you. I miss you darling; miss you more than you will ever know. Make ready sweetheart because someday soon, I will come to join you, and once again we will be together in heaven. Merry Christmas Judy, I love you.*

More than those present in the parlor saw the proposal. From the corner of the house, looking sideways to the window, the eyes saw it all. This was something he had not figured on. This would make his job easier than pie. The happy little family picture was soon to be dashed to the ground, he thought. Still, the time was not right. There was more to do to prepare. And so, the eyes turned away from the happy little scene at the school and headed back from whence they originated this morning. Soon, very soon, his time would come.

THE END

Thank you for this reading book. If you have enjoyed this book, and I hope you have, please leave a review on your favorite bookstore website. Also be sure to look for the sequel that will continue the story of Fern and her trials and tribulations in a bygone world. Due out soon!!